ABOUT THE AUTHORS

USA TODAY bestselling author **Jill Shalvis** is the author of more than three dozen award-winning romance novels. Visit www.jillshalvis.com for a complete book list and a daily blog chronicling her I-Love-Lucy attempts at having it all—the writing, the kids, a life....

A Waldenbooks bestselling author, two-time RITA® Award nominee and *RT Book Reviews* Reviewers' Choice nominee, **Rhonda Nelson** has more than twenty-five published books to her credit and many more coming down the pike. In addition to a writing career she has a husband, two adorable kids, a black Lab, and a beautiful bichon frise. She and her family make their chaotic but happy home in a small town in northern Alabama. She loves to hear from her readers, so be sure and check her out at www.readRhondaNelson.com.

Karen Foley is an incurable romantic. When she's not working for the Department of Defense, she's writing sexy romances with strong heroes and happy endings. She lives in Massachusetts with her husband and two daughters, and enjoys hearing from her readers. You can find out more about her by visiting www.karenefoley.com.

Jill Shalvis
Rhonda Nelson, Karen Foley

BORN ON THE 4TH OF JULY

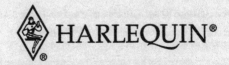

TORONTO • NEW YORK • LONDON
AMSTERDAM • PARIS • SYDNEY • HAMBURG
STOCKHOLM • ATHENS • TOKYO • MILAN • MADRID
PRAGUE • WARSAW • BUDAPEST • AUCKLAND

ISBN-13: 978-0-373-79553-6

BORN ON THE 4TH OF JULY
Copyright © 2010 by Harlequin Books S.A.

The publisher acknowledges the copyright holders
of the individual works as follows:

FRIENDLY FIRE
Copyright © 2010 by Jill Shalvis

THE PRODIGAL
Copyright © 2010 by Rhonda Nelson

PACKING HEAT
Copyright © 2010 by Karen Foley

Please Recycle — This product is recyclable

Recycling programs
for this product may
not exist in your area.

CONTENTS

FRIENDLY FIRE
Jill Shalvis

LEXI MCGOWEN stripped naked, bit her lip against the knowledge that she was trespassing and stepped into Cord Madden's shower.

Uninvited.

She told herself it wasn't breaking and entering if she had a key. It wasn't sneaking either, not really, not when she'd been bringing in his mail every day anyway since she lived in the condo right next door. And it wasn't rude—

Well, okay, it was a little rude to break into her best friend's place. It was just that her own showerhead had broken. She could have waited for a plumber, but the truth was that she was also here because—

She missed Cord, so very much. It was a little kernel of an ache that wouldn't go away, so she used the broken showerhead as an excuse to be here in his space, to stand here and inhale his scent and feel a little closer to him.

She couldn't help it, he'd been gone so long.

Too long.

She cranked the water to steamy hot and told herself that Cord wouldn't mind. He was army, Special Forces, actually, and was probably off saving the world. And, she hoped, keeping himself safe while he was at it, because for weeks now she'd been having bad dreams about him, to the point that sleep was getting to be a rare commodity.

Coming here, being in his place, gave her a small sense of peace. He'd be okay. He'd been gone this long before and he always came home okay.

She played with the showerhead, which turned out to be a miracle of engineering. Removing the nozzle, she ran it over her body. The sound of her own low, soft moan shocked her as it echoed off the tiles. She'd had no idea what she'd been missing. Heaven. This was heaven on earth. Adding to that sense was the scent of Cord's soap. She could almost feel him in here with her.

Did he do this, did he run the massager over his gorgeous, hard, leanly muscled body? The thought gave her more than a tingle and she got warm in places that hadn't been warmed in far too long. She moaned again, realizing she was completely overstepping the "friend" code, the invisible boundaries Cord had given her when he'd handed her his key eight months ago and asked her to keep an eye on his place during his fourth tour of duty. But truthfully, her mind had violated the friend code long ago, when her heart had first stepped over the "friend" line.

He didn't know it. She intended that he would never know it, mostly because she wasn't ready for those feelings anyway. She might feel guilty about not telling him, but standing there with his handheld massaging showerhead, Lexi was far closer to orgasmic bliss than guilt. Of course that might have been because she hadn't had sex in months—her own fault. She worked alone on the early shift at a grocery store designing and putting together floral arrangements for the convenience of their shoppers, and was gone before most of them ever even woke up. Hard to meet potential dates that way.

That's not why you're single, a little voice deep inside

her whispered. *You're single because beyond the occasional mutually gratifying sexual release, you aren't interested and haven't been since losing Brad three years ago now.*

Oh, yeah. *That.* She closed her eyes. Except now—with Cord—only he was gone so much.

The strategically aimed water was making her body come alive. Maybe she wasn't ready to face what she was feeling for Cord, but her body was most definitely ready to be rocked again.

If only Cord could do the rocking. Just the thought took her body from warm to hot, and she promised herself if she ever had the opportunity to be naked with him, in or out of this shower, with or without the showerhead from heaven, she'd take it.

Standing surrounded by the steamy heat, her body being gently pummeled by the delicious sting of the pulsing water, felt a little decadent, and no matter how she rationalized it, a whole lot forbidden. She soaped up, then ran the water over her shoulders, which shuddered in pleasure. When she got to her breasts, her nipples hardened. Lower still, and the muscles in her belly quivered—

When the hot water rained on her thighs, they trembled, too, and then in between—

Yowza.

It all felt so good, the water drumming out a beat on her heated flesh, the scent of Cord's body wash on her limbs, fooling her brain into believing that he could be right here with her.

Touching her.

Kissing her.

Filling her—

Five minutes ago she'd been a shower-massage virgin, and now here she was, losing that virginity with another moan and then a soft cry, which she tried but failed to bite back as she slumped against the tiled wall, unable to hold herself upright as she rode out the unexpected orgasm.

Talk about pent-up tension—

The shower door flew open, and Lexi squealed in shock, making her jerk to try to cover herself. Her arm came up with the nozzle, spraying the intruder in the face and chest.

Except it wasn't an intruder at all. "Cord," she gasped.

He stood there, nearly unrecognizable to her. And not just because he now had water dripping from his hair and the tip of his nose and chin. He was just over six feet of solid muscle and testosterone on any given day, but always when he came back from one of his missions, that sinew and innate maleness came with a tough, dangerous edge, at least until he decompressed.

Given the almost feral look in his dark eyes now, the tight jaw, the lines of grimness around his mouth—not to mention the tense way he held his body—he hadn't yet even begun the decompression process. He wore fatigue cargoes and an army-green T-shirt tight to his biceps and broad chest, loose over his flat belly. His dark hair was even shorter than his usual military short, revealing a fresh scar that cut from his left temple nearly to his jaw. He was leaning on crutches, his wide shoulders slightly hunched, exhaustion seeping from his every pore.

Her heart twisted and ached—for him, for whatever he'd had to see and do and be, and God—God, she'd missed him.

He hadn't moved a muscle since he'd opened the shower, not even to blink. Instead he stared at her as she stood before him, nozzle in hand, naked, dripping wet, body still quivering from her own decompression process.

"You're home," she whispered, her joy at seeing him

tempered by the gut-wrenching proof that he'd been injured. "And you're hurt."

His gaze lifted from the showerhead in her hands, ran briefly but heatedly over her flushed body, and then he shook his head as though he hadn't heard her because he couldn't quite believe the situation in front of him.

She couldn't either. "I was just…"

Leaning forward past her, he turned off the shower with a quick flick of his wrist.

She stared at his back, watching his muscles flex and bunch beneath his shirt as he moved, and felt the heat of embarrassment. "I'm sorry. My shower's broken. Well, not the shower, but the shower*head,* and yours is—" Perfect. "Not broken," she finished lamely. "I didn't think you'd mind, since mine can't be fixed until tomorrow, and—and never mind," she said, shaking her head at herself for babbling. "You're home. And you're hurt! What happened?"

Straightening back up, he handed her a towel and met her gaze. "What are you doing?"

She blinked. Had he not heard a thing she'd just said? "I just told you—" And then it hit her—he couldn't hear her clearly, if at all. The knowledge had her heart drumming again, dully now, in worry and fear for him. "My shower's broken," she repeated carefully.

And I missed you…

His eyes never left her lips. "Broken?"

"Yes. The showerhead— Cord," she managed past her burning throat. "Are you okay?"

Again his gaze left her mouth, running slowly down, then back up as she worked to wrap the towel around her body with hands that still shook, which meant it took longer than it should have. When she looked at him again, his eyes were closed, his jaw tight.

"I'll wait for you out there," he said, and struggled to

the door, making what appeared to be a very painful exit from the bathroom without another word.

CORD STAGGERED into the hallway. His back hit the wall next to the bathroom door and he used it to prop himself up, for the first time in three weeks not feeling any pain. Nope, all he could feel was the blood flowing out of his brain for parts south. Leaning his head back, he took a slow, deep breath. It didn't help.

Lexi naked.

Lexi wet and naked.

Lexi wet and naked and gorgeous.

Pleasuring herself.

Jesus.

He swiped a shaky hand over his face.

The bathroom door opened and a glowing, dewy Lexi peeked out, wearing nothing but his towel wrapped around her body. Her auburn hair tumbled in wet wavy strands just past her shoulders. "Cord." She looked him directly in the eyes, clearly having caught on that he needed to read her lips.

"Tell me what happened to you. Talk to me."

He shook his head. Not going there. Not least because he was so unbelievably turned on by the sight of her, his good friend, his neighbor, a woman who trusted him enough to borrow his shower, that he couldn't speak.

Worry etched lines in her face and propelled her forward to him, until she could set a hand on his chest. "Cord? Please?" Her fingers moved over him.

He let go of one of the crutches propping him upright and wrapped his hand around her wrist. "Don't."

"Don't touch you, or don't ask what happened?"

"Yes."

She hesitated, then slowly ran her gaze down his body,

stopping at the obvious erection straining the front of his cargoes.

He gritted his back teeth. "It's not what you think."

"Really?" She laughed softly and actually reached out with her free hand to touch. She nearly accomplished it, too, but he managed to drop his other crutch and, leaning his full weight against the wall, captured both of her hands.

"Christ, Lexi. You were in my shower." He shook his head, which didn't help clear it. "You were— You looked… amazing," he finished softly. "It's just my body reacting to normal stimulus after a long dry spell."

"It's a pretty spectacular reaction," she murmured throatily.

"It's my first… reaction since surgery," he heard himself admit. "So you'll have to give me a moment."

"Surgery?"

"I'm fine."

Her gaze ran down his clearly *not*-fine body. "But—"

Something in his face must have warned her, and she nibbled on her bottom lip. After a beat, she took the last step between them and rubbed her towel-clad body up against his own. Her moss-green eyes were luminous, filled with both concern and a sexuality that made him close his. "Lexi. We're just friends."

"Your reaction to seeing me naked says otherwise."

"I said we're friends, not that I was dead." He took in her beautiful face, her creamy skin, the way her breasts strained against the towel, and found his hands on her shoulders. God, she felt so good, and it'd been so long since he'd been touched by a woman's hand. And this wasn't just any woman either.

Lexi—

He pressed into her, rubbing his "reaction" up against the crux of her thighs.

"So you're...*enjoying* your first hard-on," she murmured.

"Let's just say I'm not in a hurry to scare it off," he admitted, letting his cheek brush her hair. When his fingers trailed down her arms, she shivered but stepped back. Holding his gaze, she slowly pulled the corner of the towel from between her breasts.

"Lexi—"

"We've been friends, Cord. Good friends. Let's try something else to go with." Loosened, the towel unraveled from her body and dropped to the floor.

The breath whooshed right out of Cord's lungs. Any blood that his brain had managed to retain quickly drained in a flash flood, leaving him light-headed. She was soft and curvy and gorgeous.

"Consider me your welcome-home present," she said, holding his gaze. "Welcome home."

2

LEXI WATCHED Cord's eyes darken as he looked at her standing naked in front of him. He took his time, too, taking all of her in slowly, heatedly.

"Lexi," he breathed again, his voice so low on the register it was barely audible. It was so sexy her knees wobbled.

Shaking his head, he backed her to the opposite wall. Unsteady on his feet, he nearly fell, taking her down with him, but managed to get a grip on her. "Fuck," he muttered, clearly embarrassed, and tried to pull away.

No. He was her best friend, and she'd missed him and worried about him and hoped for him…and now he was back and she couldn't let go. She knew if she did, if they shoved this under the carpet as they'd been doing with their feelings for a while now, that it would forever be awkward between them, too awkward to fix. Refusing to allow that, she grabbed him, flinging her arms around him to hold them both steady. She had no idea how bad his injuries were, what had happened to him, or even how long he'd be here. All she knew was that he was obviously hurting, and if she could take it away, even for a second, she would. "Stay."

"Lexi—"

"Stay." And then she kissed him.

He went still as stone for a single heartbeat, and then it was as if a dam burst. He pressed her hard into the wall, leaning on her, one hand bracing himself, the other on her jaw. His mouth took over, deepening their connection, stroking her tongue with his, taking her lips in a possessive, hard, wet kiss that took her to another plane entirely.

Or maybe that was his hand, skimming down her throat to her breast, his fingers grazing her nipple. Her knees wobbled, and so did his, and this time she let the momentum take them both down to the floor.

THEY HIT HARD, his own clumsy fault, and Cord's heart landed in his throat. Ignoring the pain shooting up his leg, he reached for Lexi. "Are you okay?"

Proving she was, she crawled into his lap to straddle him. His eyes went straight to the apex of her thighs, and from his position, it was a hell of a view.

It rocked his world. She rocked his world. "Lexi, you— *Jesus*," he managed in a raw voice, finding his hands on her bare arms. Gripping her hard, pulling her closer.

"Wait." She tugged his shirt over his head and then bent to kiss his throat. When she dipped even lower, licking his collarbone, a nipple, he hissed in a breath as his hands came up and fisted in her still-wet hair. "You shouldn't be here," he grated out, trying to make himself let go of her, but his hands only tightened. "I shouldn't have come home—"

"But I am. And you did."

He swore roughly, and in the next beat, he claimed her mouth again, the kiss belying his own words. God, he was in deep here. Her eyes were twin pools of jade waters, and he was drowning in them. It'd been so long, so damn long, since he'd felt anything like this. For weeks, it'd been nothing but pain and agony, both physical and mental, and then, flying home, finally numbness.

But now, on the damn floor no less, he was feeling again. Because of Lexi. Torn between a terror that he'd screw this up and lose their friendship, and a need so strong it was blinding, he held her tight, too tight, not even realizing until she cupped his face, stroking his jaw, soothing him with soft words he couldn't quite catch and the gentle movement of her body.

"It's okay, it's okay," she was murmuring, his brain finally making sense of her words, and then her mouth shifted down his chest, her busy hands undoing his cargoes. And then, oh, Christ, and then she wrapped her fingers around him. She lifted up to her knees, then sank down on him, bringing him home.

They both cried out, and he held on to her for dear life, the need for her filling him, shaking him to the core. How was it that this felt so—powerful? He'd known how important she was to him, but this went beyond what he'd imagined he could feel.

That it was her, someone so integral to his life, made him feel it all the more intense. Urging her closer, over him, his lips went to her breast, sucking her nipple into his mouth. He felt her pant for breath above him as he slid a hand down her belly to where they were joined, finding her wet, God, so wet for him. Stroking a finger over her core, absorbing her rough gasp of pleasure, he tried to thrust up into her, needing to be deeper, needing to move, but a sharp pain shot up his leg, stilling him, and in frustration, he shook his head. "I can't— I—"

"It's okay. I can." And before he knew it, she'd shifted, allowing him deeper inside her. Using his body as leverage, she began to move on him, again and again, until the pleasure pinnacled, until he couldn't see anything but her face, couldn't feel anything but her silky heat as she let go with a cry that reached into him, and he followed her over, pulsing powerfully within her.

FOR LONG MOMENTS they remained tangled in a pile of damp, sated limbs. Lexi tried to take a deep breath, and couldn't. Her heart had swelled, blocking her lungs from getting air.

Damn. She'd had no idea it would feel like that with him. She was still trembling with the little aftershocks, and so was he. She could feel them reverberate from his big body to hers.

"Jesus," he finally breathed on a shaky sigh, stroking a hand up her back. He didn't seem inclined to move, which was fine with her. She was still clinging to him, her arms tight around his neck, her face buried in his throat, basking in the scent and feel of him, the rush of joy and gratitude that he was back, if not quite whole, at least safe.

Eventually, Cord lifted his head, cupping hers so that she had to do the same. He started to say something, except he then stopped and, with a little shake of his head, kissed her instead.

It was a great kiss, another of his holy mother of all kisses, and she was well on her way to round two, her head already ringing—

Wait.

Correction. Not her head, but his cell phone. "Cord."

He was kissing and nibbling his way to her ear. Sinking her fingers in his hair, she lifted his face to hers. "Your cell phone."

"Ignore it." He went back to lightly biting her throat, soothing the sting with hot, wet, open-mouthed kisses.

She was happy to ignore everything but him, but then the house phone started ringing, and again she lifted his head. "Your land line."

With a rough oath, he let her slip off. She handed him his crutches, then bent once again for the towel, not missing his harsh groan at the view she gave him as she did. She smiled at him as she began to wrap herself up. "You want me to get it?"

"No."

"Maybe it's important."

He sighed and, using his crutches, began to make his way down the hall, only to stop and snatch the towel from her first. With a wicked gleam in his eye, he headed toward his bedroom and the ringing phone.

"Hey," she called after him. "Butt-ass naked here."

But whether he couldn't hear her or just chose not to, he kept going.

CORD STOOD in his bedroom, leaning against the windowsill, staring out at the beach.

Santa Rey had been his home all his life. Well, up until he'd gone into the army, but even then, he'd come in and out in between missions whenever he could. His two brothers were here in town, one a detective, one in the air force, which still amused him when he thought about it.

The Madden brothers, now saving the world instead of doing their damnedest to destroy it as they had when they'd been younger.

Austin and Jacob wanted to save *him* now...

Lexi came into view, moving to where he could clearly see her. She was quick. She'd already learned he couldn't hear shit, and was adjusting for him.

He hated that.

To spite him for taking her towel, she'd covered up the most beautiful body he'd ever seen with a knit T-shirt and a pair of shorts. A damn shame. He'd wanted to stare at her all day, wanted to touch again, and taste and bury himself deep…

But it was Lexi. Lexi, who brought in his mail when he wasn't home and made him food when he was. Lexi, who dated soft computer techs and laughed at him for dating bimbos. He lifted a hand and touched her pretty hair, wrapping a finger in one of the loose auburn waves he loved so much. Then he ran it over the slight shadow beneath one of her eyes. She wasn't sleeping again.

And he'd taken her on the goddamned floor.

"Who called?" she asked before he could question her about her obvious exhaustion.

"Jacob. And Austin." And twenty other concerned family members and friends. "About what just happened," he said, needing to get this out between them. "I shouldn't have—"

"Why?" She smiled. "We're good at it. If I'd known just how good, maybe it would have happened sooner."

His body twitched. No, it wouldn't have. "We're… friends."

Her eyes flickered with amusement at his obvious erection.

"Fine, I'm hard." *Again.* "But I can think with both heads." He drew a breath. "We've always been friends, Lexi. You've been there for me. And I was there for you when Brad—"

Again with the flicker of emotion across her face, this one not amusement. She didn't like thinking about the fiancé she'd lost to Hodgkin's disease two weeks before their wedding. It had been a horrible, tragic shock that had only added to her fear of losing those close to her. She'd had a lot of loss, far too much. And that fear made her worry about him, more than she should.

He hated that, hated that he caused her pain.

"I know you've always been there for me, Cord. After my parents died. After Brad. Always."

"If we take this past that friendship," he said quietly, feeling the weight of what he meant to her, even knowing she meant at least as much to him, "we might lose it.

"And then there's the fact that I have nothing to offer a woman right now. Nothing," he repeated when she opened her mouth to speak.

She looked at him in that way she had of making him feel like a bug on a slide. Like she could see everything she needed to see no matter how he tried to hide it, and he braced for the questions.

But she neither said nor asked a thing of him.

"I'm sorry if I misled you," he finally said.

"You didn't. You couldn't."

"Lexi." He let out a slow breath, hating the hurt beneath her words. "What do you want to hear?"

"Whatever you can tell me."

Fair enough. "For starters, I've been put on disability as of two weeks ago."

"Is your hearing loss permanent? Your leg in danger?"

"Don't know on the hearing. No on the leg. But..." Might as well tell her. "My team, my brothers, friends, hell, everyone I know is feeling sorry for me and walking on eggshells thinking I'm on the edge getting ready to jump."

"Are you?"

"Only if one more person offers me a single goddamn ounce of pity."

She was quiet.

A miracle. One that made him want to rip her clothes off and lose himself again.

"I'm starving," she finally said. "Want to call for a pizza?"

3

"A PIZZA," Cord said, repeating Lexi's words as if he couldn't possibly have heard her correctly.

"Yeah." She could feel the tension and frustration pouring off him in waves. She understood it wasn't directed at her. She understood a lot about anger, actually. Too much. She'd felt it after losing her parents. She'd felt it after losing Brad. "A pizza. Large, fully loaded?"

He just stared at her.

He'd lost weight. He'd always been built like a kickboxer, tightly muscled, and though he was still solid sinew, there wasn't a spare ounce on him, as if he'd been burning far more calories than he'd been taking in. He was also clearly in pain, and she'd never been able to resist anything in pain. "Cord?"

His gaze was slowly running down her body again, giving her more thrills on what had turned out to be a high-thrill day.

"Are you still on the pill?" he questioned.

"Now's a fine time to ask."

"I'm sorry. I—" He shook his head and then rubbed his temples as if exhausted, beyond exhausted, and she would have melted, but he'd already melted her completely.

"I'm on the pill," she reassured him. Not that she'd even given a single thought to birth control once he'd touched her...

"I'm sorry," he said again.

She knew he was apologizing both for the fact that he'd been so lost in her he hadn't thought of it either, and that it'd even happened in the first place. "I'm not," she said frankly.

He let out a breath.

"So. Pizza?" she asked.

"Yeah." He used his crutches to move in her direction, his movements painfully labored.

Her fingers itched to help but she forced herself to remain still. "Cord?"

"Yeah?"

She kept her smile easy and light, even though her heart was not either of those things. "I missed you." It was true. When he wasn't on a tour of duty, they spent a lot of time together, swimming, surfing, running, even just sitting around watching TV. They had a closeness born from years of being friends, and being there for each other through thick and thin. "A lot."

He let out a slow breath, his gaze never leaving hers. "I missed you, too."

She held her smile until he turned and made his way down the hall to the living room, then let it fall from her lips.

God. What had happened to him?

She moved back into the bathroom and quickly finger-combed her hair, the best she could do at the moment. Barefoot, she padded down the hall after Cord, slowing when she realized he stood, his back to her, his cell on speaker, volume earsplitting as he listened to his messages.

"Cord, Jesus. You left the hospital without a word." The

voice belonged to his brother, Jacob Madden, a Santa Rey undercover detective, a guy as big and tough and badass as Cord himself. "You shouldn't be alone. Call me or I'm coming over."

Cord hit a button. Message deleted.

Next message. "Cord, where the hell are you, man?" This was his other brother, Austin, also big and bad, and currently on leave from the air force. "Jacob's shitting a brick. Call me."

Message deleted.

The next message came up before Lexi could make herself known. "Cord, baby, honey, I told you I'd stay with you." This voice, sweetly female, sounded breathy. "I took the week off to take care of your every…little…*need*."

"Damn." This was from Cord himself as he again hit Delete.

As Lexi walked around to where he could see her, he began wrestling with a low cabinet beneath the bar. "Cord?" she whispered on his right and slightly behind him.

He didn't react.

She moved to his left side, still back out of sight. "Cord," she said loudly, and he turned his head and looked at her as he pulled out a phone book.

"Yeah?"

"Nothing." Except he still had hearing in his left ear, at least some. She didn't ask him about it. She knew sure as she knew her own name that he most definitely wasn't ready to talk about it.

And after hearing his messages, she understood some of his anger. Everyone wanted to baby the hell out of him, and his pride couldn't take it.

Something else she understood.

Hadn't her own family and friends tried to do the same

thing for her when Brad had died? Everyone but Cord. Cord had given her the space and time she'd needed to heal.

He opened the phone book, trying to balance himself on one crutch. She was dying to help but, as if he knew it, he sent her a narrow-eyed glare. She simply smiled. "Do you want to get a salad, too?" she asked.

He paused. "Sure." Flipping open his cell again, he began punching on the keypad.

"What are you doing?"

He didn't answer her, so she moved around the edge of the bar and into the kitchen, on his left side. He looked up, and for one beat she could see he was startled that she'd moved without him knowing it.

Startled and frustrated.

She ignored that, even as her heart tightened for him, hard. "What are you doing?"

"Texting in the order. Drink?"

"I have beer at my place." She had a feeling they both needed it.

He finished the order, closed his phone, slid it into his pocket and stood at the bar, leaning heavily on it.

He needed to sit before he fell. Prone would probably be even better. She was certain he needed sleep, days of it, but hell if she'd mother him and allow him to lump her in with the rest of his family and friends, so she just waited him out.

"What?" he finally asked.

"Nothing."

"It's something."

Yeah, it was. Something big. "How long will you be home?"

He turned his back on her and maneuvered his way to the couch. "Probably permanently."

Her heart leaped. "What?" Following, she planted herself in front of him. *"What?"*

"I've been cut loose." He shrugged his broad shoulders in a casual gesture that wasn't casual. Cord *was* his work. Being in the army had been his entire life.

"Apparently," he said, "my team actually needs me to be able to hear them on the equipment, not to mention being able to maneuver around without stumbling."

That's when she got it. He wasn't just frustrated and angry.

He was scared.

Scared of living a life he hadn't planned on. Throat tight, she waited until he looked at her. If she said how sorry she was, he'd kick her ass out, she knew it. If she so much as offered a single beat of empathy, it'd be over. "I'm going to get the beer," she said, and forced herself to walk out the door.

THE MINUTE she was gone, Cord gave in to his quaking leg muscles and sat at a barstool. He dropped his head to the granite top and closed his eyes, letting the silence wash over him, a staggering quiet utterly devoid of anything that reminded him of the Middle East.

It'd been three weeks since all hell had broken loose on his mission. He and two others from his team had nearly been blown to bits, had certainly been blown from their Humvee. It'd taken twelve hours to get to a medical facility, during which time he'd nearly bled out because of the eighteen-inch gash in his leg.

His ears were still ringing. He had complete loss in his right ear, sixty-five-percent loss in his left. The doctors were fairly certain he'd get at least fifty percent back.

They'd been more optimistic about his leg. Lying in 105-degree heat in the dirt with his leg sliced wide open to the elements for several hours hadn't been exactly ideal, and he was lucky to still have the limb at all, but he was slowly recovering.

But his basketball-playing days were over, and so were his covert-op missions. No one wanted a gimp for a partner, and he sure as hell couldn't blame them.

But it still sucked.

He caught a flash of movement and lifted his head, expecting to see Lexi letting herself back in.

It was Jacob and Austin.

Both of his brothers had flown back east when he'd landed stateside. Not easy in their line of work. But they'd come and babysat him at the hospital until he'd been out of danger.

And then they'd remained on him like white on rice, convinced he was still in danger, this time from himself.

He was pissed.

Frustrated.

But definitely not suicidal, not even close. "Jesus," he muttered when they flanked him, sitting one on either side of him at the bar. "I'm *fine*."

Across the kitchen, the late sun slanted in the window, momentarily rendering it into a looking glass. Their three faces reflected back to Cord, all of them looking so much alike: dark hair, dark eyes, matching grim mouths. Their broad shoulders nearly touched, and Cord forced himself to push to his feet when what he really wanted was to drop his head to the bar and sleep right there on the spot.

"Come home with me," Austin said. "I've got a fully stocked refrigerator and the pool, which the doctor said would be great for rehabbing your leg—"

"I want to stay here, at my place."

"Told you," Jacob said to Austin. He looked at Cord.

"Okay, we're not asking. Pack your stubborn ass up and let's go."

Austin, the middle brother, the peacemaker, knew better. He sighed and pinched the bridge of his nose. "Jacob, when has that *ever* worked?"

Jacob wouldn't care. They were brothers, they fought more than not, but the bottom line was that they took care of each other. Always had. Cord knew that Jacob didn't see anything wrong with using strong-arm tactics to get his way.

But he wasn't going.

"There's no reason for you to be alone," Jacob tried in the low, reasonable tone that made him such a good cop. "We can—"

"I want to be alone."

They just looked at Cord, silently considering the best way to muscle him through this. And into that tense silence, Lexi sauntered back through the front door, swinging a six-pack, wearing her sweet, sexy grin.

So sexy. Cord wondered how he'd never noticed just how much until she'd come for him.

Or how long her legs were until she'd wrapped them around his hips.

Or how her eyes promised that they'd only just gotten started...

"Hi," she said, and sent his brothers a little wave. "You two joining us for pizza and beer?"

"No," Jacob said. "We're dragging his sorry ass back with us."

"No," Cord told her. "They're not."

"Cord," Austin said. "We don't want you to be alone."

"He's not." Though Lexi kept her smile in place, her eyes were on Cord, quiet and assessing. "Alone, that is. I'm here."

"Lexi," Jacob said, just as quiet and assessing. "I know you're a good friend, but knowing my knuckle-headed brother, he's underplayed his injuries. He needs daily PT, around-the-clock care, and—"

"Yes," Lexi said, nodding, her eyes still on Cord's, holding his gaze prisoner. "I understand. But it's going to be fine. He wants to be home, and I'm here."

Austin turned to Cord, shaking his head. "It's your choice, man. But—"

"I'm staying," Cord said, looking at Lexi, who nodded. "And, like she said, it's going to be fine."

"Better than fine," she said firmly. "I plan to make sure of it."

"She'll make sure of it," Cord repeated to his brothers, wishing that could involve seeing her naked again. Because that had done more for his body than anything had in weeks.

But he had to make sure it didn't happen. He had no business leading her on.

Jacob narrowed his eyes, dividing a look between Cord and Lexi. "Is something happening between you two?"

"Do we need to go over curfew time, Dad?" Cord asked drily.

As always, Austin stepped in. "I know you mean well, Lexi, but it's a huge responsibility to lay on you."

"It's what friends are for," Lexi murmured.

Right.

Friends.

They were just friends, and no matter what happened, or how many times she dropped her towel—and, how he'd loved that—they were just friends.

Unless…unless they changed their minds. No one had said they couldn't change their minds. Thing was, he didn't see her doing that. She played it cool and she played it tough. She protected herself always, and he knew she wouldn't easily let down that guard for anyone.

And he didn't know if he could let down his own guard enough to even want her to.

4

JACOB AND Austin stayed for the pizza and beer. They all watched a DVD, a comedy, and though Cord's brothers tried to talk to him about what had happened overseas, both the injuries he'd suffered and the fact that life as he'd known it was over, he remained stubbornly mute.

Lexi understood that his brothers meant well, but she also understood that Cord needed time.

Time and space.

Something she was perfectly willing to give him—to a point. Actually, she was willing to give him whatever he needed, she just happened to disagree with him on what that was. To that end, she came up with a plan. Operation Bring Cord Back to Life. She would go about it as methodically as she'd go about any task, the goal being to remind him of what he was missing out on.

ON CORD'S second day home, she brought him his mail. He looked at her and asked, "Need my showerhead again?"

I need you again, she almost said. And maybe her eyes *had* said it because he slowly shook his head. "Bad idea, Lexi."

Right. Bad idea.

But why was it that bad ideas always sounded so damn good?

"I need to be alone," he said.

"You can be alone after I'm gone."

He stood there glowering, but she set her hands lightly on his abs—Lord, those abs!—and gently pushed him aside, letting herself in.

He sighed and followed her to the couch. They watched a *24* repeat on TV and when an explosion rocked Jack Bauer's world, Cord turned off the TV and tossed the remote aside.

Silence.

She took his hand, and he let her. "You're alive," she said loudly into the quiet afternoon, and squeezed his fingers. "You can recover from anything if you're alive."

He absorbed that a moment, running his thumb over her palm. "Question is, where do I go from here?"

"You spend the time recovering before deciding that." But looking into his face, seeing the frustration and the vulnerability she was quite certain he didn't mean to project, her heart squeezed. "You'll find something else to do that will fulfill you the same way saving the world did."

He closed his eyes.

Apparently he was done talking.

Time and space, she reminded herself. And her plan, with its goal.

With that goal in mind, Lexi brought Cord lunch and his mail every day after her shift at work, pretty much bullying her way into his life, getting him to his appointments, driving him to the store, being a general pain in his ass, but at least getting him up and out.

Every single time she appeared, he was no friendlier than he'd been the time before, but she was wearing him down, she could tell.

Actually, more accurately, he probably allowed her in because she wasn't taking no for an answer. She was a bulldog.

Everyone else he knew was treading gently and treating him like a cracked egg. She knew this because she was around him enough to hear all his high-decibel phone conversations.

At night, his brothers came over with dinner, and usually stayed past Lexi's bedtime. Not difficult, since she went to bed early to get up before the crack of dawn for work. Which meant that there'd been no more chances for additional naked incidents.

Darn it.

On Cord's third day back, Lexi had brought him the usual—his mail and lunch, plus two Popsicles. Cord watched as she sat next to him on the couch where he'd been on his laptop. He took a Popsicle and almost smiled. "Grape?"

"Yep."

"What are we, five?"

She sucked her Popsicle into her mouth and his eyes darkened. He had no more comments.

They sucked in silence awhile, and then Lexi asked him what was wrong. Besides the obvious.

"I'm so fucking bored all the time."

"Means you're healing."

He shook his head. "I thought of you this morning at the crack of dawn and I almost waited by your car to beg you to take me with you to work. And I don't know a daisy from a lily." He let out a breath. "I don't know what to do with myself."

"You do whatever you want, Cord. What do you want?"

His eyes followed the path of her tongue as it circled her

Popsicle, and suddenly she could barely breathe. Oh, boy, what she hoped he wanted… "Jacob works for the P.D.," she said. "Maybe you could, too."

He arched a surprised brow.

"What?" she asked.

"Every damn person I know wants me to sit on my ass for the rest of my life and be safe, my brothers included. And yet you suggest another dangerous job." He smiled. And good Lord, it was a beauty. "You're different, Lexi."

"Different bad or different good?"

He just looked at her some more, those eyes smoldering. "I can't answer, on the grounds it might incriminate me."

He was flirting with her…

She was afraid to point that out, afraid to scare him off, but something deep inside her tightened. If he could flirt, he really was feeling better.

The next afternoon she brought him a stack of games and made him play. They started with Pictionary, and she actually made him laugh at her stick drawings. A full-bellied laugh that stopped her heart and filled it with warmth. "How was physical therapy?" she asked.

He shrugged, the same answer she'd gotten in the car earlier when she'd dropped him off at home. She knew his physical therapist had him working on losing the crutches and graduating to a cane. "You putting weight on the leg?"

"Yeah. With a fucking cane."

"That's great!"

"Old guys use a cane, Lexi."

"Hey, a cane can be sexy. It's all in how you wield it."

He gave her a long look. "You think a cane is sexy."

No, she thought *he* was sexy. In anything. "Can we be done talking about your cane woes now? I have a real dilemma. Brownies or cookies for dessert?"

A WEEK LATER, Lexi found him alone in his yard, a big, bad, hurting ex-special ops soldier lying inclined on a lounge, brooding off into the distance. The scent of the sea air brushed over her and she watched as it ruffled Cord's short dark hair and flirted with the T-shirt stretched tautly across his chest.

He was staring at the ocean, unnaturally still, and she worried that his PT had pushed him too hard again. Because, God knew, Cord was so stubborn he'd work until he was dead if it meant healing faster. With a deep breath, she moved across the grass and came to a stand in front of him.

He didn't budge.

"Cord," she said softly, and put her other hand to his arm.

He launched out of the chair, his hand on her wrist in a death grip tight enough that he could have snapped it like a twig if he'd tried.

It took him less than a second to register who she was and let go of her as if she was a hot potato. Staggering backward, off balance since his cane was on the ground, he sank to the lounge. "Did I hurt you?"

"I'm tougher than you might think." She smiled, but he didn't.

He turned away, clearly pissed, but she knew that his anger was directed at himself, not her. Which left her in a quandary. She stared at his broad back, wanting to hug the hell out of him and never let go. She wanted to hug away his suffering, his pain and the horrific memories, but he'd hate that.

So she went in another direction. First she moved to where he could see her, then handed him an ice cream sandwich. Silently, he took it. "Where's yours?"

"I already ate it."

He almost smiled at that, she could tell. He took a bite, then offered her one, as well. Putting her hand over his, she bent in close and took a lick at the vanilla ice cream squeezing out through the chocolate biscuits.

His eyes went black.

Liking the change in him from bad tension to a sexual one, she licked again.

His eyes carefully followed the movement, shooting flames now. "Lexi."

His voice was that low sexy rasp that always made her nipples hard. "Yes?" she managed.

"What are you doing?"

"Distracting you. Is it working?"

He looked at her halter top, at the way her nipples were poking against the fabric. "Little bit."

Holy smokes. "So. Is this today's plan?" she asked casually, telling herself not to notice how he looked in his threadbare jeans, but, oh, God help her, those jeans! "Sleeping away the day?"

He said nothing.

"I thought maybe that would be getting old by now."

More nothing.

"Because I came over here to see if you wanted to go to the beach and bodysurf, but hey, if you're going to be lazy…"

He looked at her in silent disbelief. "Bodysurfing," he repeated slowly, and she couldn't blame him. But she refused to let him give up. So he couldn't be a badass special ops guy anymore. There were other things.

"I can barely stand," he pointed out. "I think it's safe to say bodysurfing isn't in my near future."

"How about just floating in the water, out past the waves?" They'd done that together before, plenty of times. He swam like a fish. He also looked damn good in his board shorts, which was a sight she'd like to see again. "Have you tried it? Come on," she said, and stood, hands on hips. "Get up."

"Lexi."

She clucked like a chicken and he stared at her in shock. "You think I'm *afraid?*"

Alpha men and their fear of admitting fear. "Are you?" she challenged.

"Jesus." He scrubbed a hand down his face. But he reached for his cane, made his painful way to his feet and glared at her. "You used to be nice."

She smiled. "Still am. Nice and sweet."

"I'll give you the nice, since you've been feeding me all week. But sweet ..." He looked her over from her freshly manicured red toenails peeking out of her sandals to her little board shorts and halter top, all chosen with him in mind today. Not that she wanted him to notice her as a woman.

Okay, she wanted him to notice her as a woman.

But mostly she just wanted to help him feel good. She wanted him to relax and enjoy himself.

She wanted to see him smile, hear him laugh.

"I don't know about sweet," he said, a new quality to his voice now, a husky, lower tone that brought to mind hot-summer-night sex.

Setting a hand on his chest, she smiled. "I am *very* sweet."

He wrapped his fingers around her hand and brought it up to his mouth, kissing the inside of the wrist he'd inadvertently squeezed only a moment ago.

Her breath caught at the feel of his warm lips on her skin.

Eyes still on hers, he then kissed her palm and touched his tongue to the spot.

Holy mother of God. She had to lock her knees. "Wh-what are you doing?"

"Tasting you." He spoke against her flesh. "You're right. You are sweet, Lexi. So damn sweet."

She found herself staring at his mouth, and then somehow it was on hers, and they were kissing madly, fiercely, trying to crawl into each other's skin. The sound of his cane clattering to the patio startled them apart.

Breathing unsteadily, she stared at him, only slightly gratified to see he wasn't breathing so lightly either. She rubbed up against his impressive erection. "Are you having a difference of opinion with your favorite body part again?"

"Lexi," he said, sounding tortured.

"Right." She nodded. "We're not going there."

He didn't say anything on the walk to the beach, and Lexi let him have his silence. As she'd hoped, he'd changed into his board shorts. They were sky-blue and rested low enough on his hips to reveal every inch of his incredible eight-pack stomach, and more than a hint of what lay beneath.

Using his cane, he limped at her side from the condo building through the field of wild grass, then stopped, eyeing the strip of sand pensively, body tense.

She'd called his PT; she knew that maneuvering through the sand would be a bitch, but that it'd be a great exercise for him. This time she waited for him to look at her before setting a hand on his arm.

One corner of his mouth quirked, as if ruefully acknowledging that she'd at least learned to give him warning before touching him. "I'm not losing it," he said. "I'm not going postal."

"Of course you're not."

"I just want to be left alone."

"Pretend you're alone. I'll try to be quiet."

His mouth quirked again. "That would be an impossible feat."

"Ha. Come on, Cord. Let's see what you're made of." She was carrying both their body boards. She watched him struggle through the sand. Her throat tightened and her heart ached because God, it was hard, so damn hard, to watch him, to see the flash of pain pinch his features when he put his weight down wrong. But, as determined as he, she kept a smile on her face and matched her pace to his as they made their way to the water.

5

CORD STOOD at the water's edge and watched Lexi corral her wild hair into a ponytail. Then she pulled off her halter top and shorts, leaving her in an itsy-bitsy teeny-tiny bright-red bikini that nearly had him swallowing his tongue.

"Cord?"

He realized she was smiling at him, the witch, clearly pleased with his reaction.

"You coming?" she asked.

They were alone on the beach. He moved closer, so that the water lapped over his feet, then met her gaze, which was pretty much eating him up from top to bottom. "Lexi," he heard himself rumble warningly in a rough voice.

Slowly she ran a finger over his pec. "I'm your friend," she murmured. "But I'm not dead."

He stared at her as she used his own words against him, and hell if he didn't end up smiling. She flashed him one in return, then pivoted, grabbed the two boards and strode into the water.

He followed, eyes on her sweet ass as the water splashed up to her thighs and beyond. His life might be shit, but the view wasn't so shabby. He eyed the waves. Barely swells today, maybe two feet. Which was good, considering even two feet could easily kick his butt.

But hell if he was going to back down, not with Lexi already in the water, holding the boards. He dropped his cane and limped in, taking one of the boards from her.

Lexi splashed in a little farther. Water droplets dotted her red bikini, darkening it in spots.

When she turned back to check on his progress, he could see her nipples were hard. "Coming?"

He'd like to be coming… He'd like her to be coming, too, screaming his name. He put his chest to the board and dove into the next wave to clear his head and to get his weight off his leg. He came up and shook the water out of his face, and felt himself smile.

Lexi splashed his back and he turned to face her. She put a hand to his jaw and lifted his face so that he was looking at her mouth instead of at her wet breasts. "I asked how you're doing."

Fine, since the cold water swirling about him was keeping his erection down to a minimum. To think, only two weeks ago he'd been recovering from surgery wondering why he couldn't get hard, and now here he was, perpetually hard, and he had been since the night he'd gotten home and found Lexi in his shower in the throes of a self-induced orgasm.

"Cord?"

Right. She'd said something and he'd missed it, something that sounded like "go to bed"? In that moment, with the sun on his back and the gorgeous woman in that heart-stopping bikini smiling at him, he was tired of fighting the attraction. "Bed sounds good."

Her eyes widened. "What?"

Uh-oh. "Um, what?"

Her eyes narrowed. "I said, I should have brought bread.

For the seagulls." She gestured to the birds bodysurfing near them.

"Oh." *Idiot.*

"And then you said 'Bed sounds good.'"

"I said *bread* sounds good."

She wasn't buying it. "Your nose is growing."

Uh-huh, and that wasn't the only thing.

She continued to stare at him for another moment, the pause long enough for him to realize that her breathing had changed. "'Bed sounds good?'" she repeated yet again.

"Hell, Lexi. Have you seen yourself? I have sex on the brain."

Her eyes dilated. "Then let's do it. Now."

It'd be so easy to say yes.

"And then maybe after, we can talk."

"About?" he asked, sensing a trap.

"What you don't want to talk about."

Yeah, a trap. And because he was thinking about that and not what he was doing, a swell swamped him, rolling right over the top of his head. "Fuck," he said when he resurfaced.

"Yes, that's what I'm saying."

"You're crazy," he said with a laugh.

"And you're scared." She said this with terrifying gentleness. "You're scared of being useless, which is ridiculous, Cord. You're the most un-useless man I've ever met. Just think about it. I'll leave the offer on the table for as long as you need. Well, not too long. A girl has needs."

Their gazes met. He put a hand on the nape of her neck. Her skin was warm.

At his touch, she leaned in close enough to kiss him, messing with his balance and his head all at the same time before she pushed him back and smiled.

She was teasing him.

Not fussing over him.

Not babying him.

But making fun and making him laugh…and enjoying him while she was at it. She could have no idea what an incredible turn-on that was. So he returned her smile because…oh, yeah, there it was—

The wave hit her from behind. With a surprised gasp, she went down.

When she came up sputtering, he laughed.

Laughed.

A *much* better sport than he, she grinned, too, and they both lay flat on the body boards, out past the waves now, gently riding up and down on the swells.

"Nice, right?" Lexi said after a few minutes of blissful silence.

"It's the nicest time I've had since…"

Her gaze was steady on his, waiting patiently for him to say what he didn't want to say. He'd been doing his damnedest to push her away just as he did everyone else, but she didn't push. Nor did she make any concession to the fact that he couldn't hear worth shit and his leg was still all but useless.

She didn't care about any of that, she cared about him. And he was realizing that he cared back, far more than he'd meant to.

"I have sand in my parts," she said conversationally.

"Nothing a shower wouldn't cure. I volunteer my showerhead to that worthy cause. I believe you already know how to use it."

Her cheeks reddened. "I can't believe you're going to bring that up."

"My mind brings it up daily. Hourly."

"Seriously? Men really think about sex hourly?"

"I'm pretty sure it's by the minute."

She shook her head, marveling. "How do you ever get anything done?"

"Says the woman who was doing herself in my shower."

"I couldn't help it! I've never used one of those before."

Reaching out, he grabbed her board and pulled her in close again. He ran a finger over her jawline. "And let me just say, no one's ever put it to better use."

"Not even Boobs-Out-to-Here?"

He grinned at the reference to his last girlfriend. "Not even her."

She laughed, the sound soft and musical. The sun beat down on them, the light wind and lapping water keeping them cool.

"I'm having a good time, Cord."

"Me, too," he said, no longer surprised that he always did with her. Still gripping her board, he slid his other hand into her hair. Her lips met his eagerly, light at first, but as it always seemed to be with them, the connection sparked something too deep and demanding to ignore. Small brushing kisses weren't enough, not by a long shot, and, as one, they rolled off the boards and gravitated to each other in the water. Cord pulled her in close, running his tongue along her lower lip until she opened for him again.

She moaned, and he lost himself in the sensation of her, her scent, her taste, the heat of her body, the way her hands ran restlessly over him as if she couldn't get enough.

He knew the feeling. He had one hand on her breast, his thumb rubbing her pebbled nipple, the other down the back of her suit, cupping her ass. He squeezed a bare cheek, then let his fingers slide lower, discovering a creamy heat that made him groan and lose his balance in the waist-high water, staggering until she braced to help support him.

"I've got us," she murmured, sliding her hands down his back in a gesture that made him forget being weak enough to need support.

She was strong enough for both of them, inside and out. "Lexi," he murmured, and took advantage of her spread legs to touch her.

She gasped and shivered. "So you're going to talk to me, then?"

"Now?" he asked incredulously, slipping a finger inside her wet heat.

She moaned and her eyes drifted shut. "After is good."

He stared down into her beautiful, open face, wanting to agree. Christ, he wanted her so much he would agree to just about anything, except hurting her. And if he lied now, he would do exactly that. Because he didn't want to talk, he didn't want to open up. He wasn't ready for that.

She opened her eyes, saw the regret in his, and let out a breath. She pulled free, even now taking the time to make sure he could balance before she let him go. The way she did that, took care of him at all costs, had him stepping outside his own misery for the first time since the explosion and thinking of someone other than himself. He was a selfish prick, wanting just the escape. "Lexi—"

"No," she said, lifting a hand. "It's okay, Cord."

But it sure as hell didn't feel okay. Not one little bit.

THAT NIGHT, Lexi couldn't sleep. This was nothing new. The insomnia always came in cycles. When Brad had died, she'd gone months without a good night's sleep, and then Cord had started running with her late in the evenings.

The exhaustion had helped ease her back into a healthy sleeping pattern. But she didn't like to run alone, and

Cord had been gone for eight long months this time, and gradually the insomnia had crept back up on her.

It was embarrassing—the weakness, the vulnerability—and so she hid it. But that night, somewhere between one and two o'clock, she gave up the fight and kicked the covers off, walking through her dark condo for a glass of water.

In her kitchen, she saw the light reflecting from the kitchen next door.

Cord was up.

Without stopping to think, she moved out her back door and, in her camisole and boxer pj's, padded barefoot to his. He was in his kitchen, leaning against the counter, one crutch beneath an armpit—he used the crutches when he was too sore for his cane—the other hand holding a mug.

He wore only a pair of loose basketball shorts, so low on his hips as to be nearly indecent. She pictured him sleeping in the nude, and pulling those on almost as an afterthought as he walked through his condo.

His eyes were shut, his head back, exposing his throat. He was still, but she knew he wasn't asleep on his feet.

And then he unerringly cut his eyes to hers, lifting a brow as she let herself in. Her eyes snagged on his body, rangy and hard with sinew from top to bottom. "Hey," she murmured.

Without a word, he set down the mug and limped toward her, not stopping until they were toe to toe. Dipping down a little, he looked right into her eyes. "You're not sleeping again."

She looked away, but he put a hand on her jaw and brought her back. She nodded, then shrugged and grimaced.

No. She wasn't sleeping again.

He set his crutch against the counter and opened his arms.

And she moved right into them.

"How long?" he murmured, nuzzling his face into her hair.

"Couple of months."

"A couple?"

"Or eight."

He went still, then let out a low breath. "Lexi."

"It's not the same this time." She slid her hands up his smooth, sleek back and burrowed in, accepting his comfort, because damn if he didn't get her in the heart. Every single time.

"Before, it was grief," she said. A devastating grief. She and Brad had been high-school sweethearts. They'd known each other a long time. His death had left a hole in her heart and soul. But the fact was, one couldn't maintain that level of sorrow; it just wasn't possible. Slowly but surely, whether she liked it or not, she'd moved on. Moved on and…fallen in love again? "It's not like that anymore. I don't think about him as much." Sometimes she couldn't even remember his voice. "Now I just…" *Love you…?* "I think I'm just lonely."

He made a soft sound that said he knew exactly what she meant. Like maybe he got lonely, too. Taking his hand, she pulled him toward the door.

"Where are we going?" he asked.

"Well, since you haven't taken me up on my deal, we'll have to find another way to absolve our loneliness."

He let her lead him outside into the dark night. "More bodysurfing? You're in pj's, Lexi."

"We're not bodysurfing, not at 2:00 a.m., no." She opened her car door and gestured him in.

"If you get pulled over wearing that, you're going to make some cop's night."

"I'm decent enough. Get in."

In nothing but those basketball shorts, he slid into the passenger seat and shot her a look tinged with very slight amusement, but he said nothing more, letting her lead.

Which she loved about him.

She drove them out to the north bluffs. There was no one there, not a single soul, which was exactly what she'd counted on. They sat on the very edge, their feet swinging into nothingness, the waves crashing two hundred feet below against the wall of the cliff.

She studied Cord a moment, watched him looking out into the night before shifting so that he could see her. "You're even quieter tonight than you've been."

When he said nothing to this, she went on. "I think it's because, like I did over Brad, you're grieving. You're grieving the end of your career. And it sucks." And taking a deep breath, she screamed, loud and long.

He didn't jump. He didn't flinch. He just arched a brow.

She grinned. "That felt good. Your turn."

"You want me to scream at the ocean?"

"Yeah."

"To grieve the end of my military career?"

"Yeah."

He gave a little head shake, like he couldn't believe what he was going to do. And then he turned back to the water and let out a powerful yell from the top of his lungs. When he was done, he smiled.

Her smile widened. "Right?"

"Not bad," he admitted. "But I can think of a better way to make you scream."

6

CORD WATCHED Lexi as she gave him the bum's rush home. No easy task, given he had seven inches and at least fifty pounds on her. "In a hurry?"

She took a page out of his book and didn't answer. Instead, she helped him up to his front door, putting both hands on his ass and shoving him up the last step.

He grinned. "If you wanted to cop a feel, you could have just said so."

"Did you mean it?"

He didn't even try to pretend not to know what she was asking. "Did I mean it when I said I could think of a better way to make you scream?" His fingers brushed her temple, his thumb gliding over her jaw. "Hell, yes."

Her eyes flashed heat and hunger and desire, and he went instantly hard. A chronic condition around her.

She grabbed his hand and tugged him inside, then pushed him back against the door and gestured to his basketball shorts. "Lose 'em."

He choked out a laugh. "Aren't you going to buy me dinner first?"

She shot him an amused glance. "Do you need the

bells and whistles? The romance? I thought we were just friends."

His smile faded, and he slowly tugged her in, smoothing back her wild hair from her face. "Lexi."

She shook her head, and put a finger across his lips. "No. You promised to make me scream. Please don't change your mind. I know what this is, and what it isn't."

Oh, Christ, she killed him. "I want to—"

She shook her head and closed her eyes, looking suddenly unsure and vulnerable, as if maybe she expected him to turn her down.

As if he could.

"Please," she whispered, making his heart ache. "Just love me…"

I already do, he thought with no little amount of shock, but even with the unexpected epiphany, he managed to take her hand, leading her away from the foyer.

"Where are we—"

"My bed," he said firmly. "I'm too old for this against-the-door shit, and my leg is killing me."

"Oh, Cord. We don't have to—"

"We're doing this." Knowing she needed him to keep this light—which was ironic given that this had started out with *him* being the skittish one—he flashed her a grin over his shoulder. "But you'll have to promise to be gentle with me."

LEXI PROPELLED Cord onto his bed and followed him down. "Hurry," she said, mouth busy against his throat. God, he was big and warm and solid against her, and she scraped her teeth over him. "I want you in me."

He groaned and gripped her hips hard. "Is there a fire?"

She laughed breathlessly, trying to get his shorts off, but

he surprised her by rolling, tucking her beneath him. He gathered both her hands in one of his, raising them over her head as he pressed her into the mattress. "Lexi."

God, she loved the feel of him on top of her. "What?"

"I want to go slow."

"But I like fast. Like last time."

He winced. "Okay, that didn't count. It'd been a really long time for me and—"

"Cord, it was perfect." She wrapped her legs around him. "Now do it again."

"I'm going to. But I want to touch you, Lexi. Taste you—"

"So get to it!"

He dropped his forehead to hers and let out a sound that was a cross between a groan and a laugh. She slid her hands into his shorts, wrapped her fingers around his length and ran her thumb over the tip of him, humming in approval at finding him so satisfyingly hard.

He let out another rough sound, this one completely void of amusement. "You really want fast?"

"And hard."

"Everything off, then," he demanded, and then lent his hands to the cause, ripping off their pj's. Before she drew another breath, he'd nudged her legs apart and slid home.

She opened her lips to gasp in shocked pleasure, but he thrust his tongue into her mouth for a long, searching kiss as he began to move within her, slow smooth strokes that had her heart pounding, her desire for him consuming her from the inside out.

"God, you feel good." Dipping down so he could see into her face, he balanced up on one forearm to stroke her damp hair back. "So damn good."

So did he, and she nodded, closing her eyes. She wanted the big bang, the explosion, the mindless pleasure, needed it. Wrapping her thighs around his waist, she dug her fingers into his perfect butt and met him thrust for thrust.

He groaned, running hot, wet, open-mouthed kisses down her throat and back up, covering her mouth with his, making her toes curl. When he murmured her name again in a voice that told her he was close, she finally let go of the nameless tension that had her in its tight-fisted grip and burst as wave after wave of pleasure crashed over her, carrying him right along with her.

FROM THE BED, they staggered into Cord's kitchen for water. Lexi's throat was parched, and she was downing a glass when she realized Cord was watching her with hot eyes. They were both still naked, their bodies barely cool, but God, the way he was looking at her made her knees wobble.

He held the eye contact as he limped toward her. Lifting her to the countertop, he stroked his hands down her already quivering body.

"Again?" she murmured, breath catching.

"Oh, yeah," he murmured back, voice low and sexy as hell. "Again."

AFTER THE KITCHEN, where they managed to incorporate several cooking utensils and a quart of ice cream into their lovemaking, they made their way to Cord's shower, where, as it turned out, the magical showerhead was even more fun with two.

She currently had Cord flat on his back on the bathroom floor, and she was riding him like a wild bronco. She couldn't help herself, she couldn't get enough of him....

His eyes dark on hers, he let loose his grip on her hip to stroke his thumb over her center, which was all it took for her to go flying again, his name on her lips.

It might even have been that scream he'd promised her, and when she let go, he arched, burying himself even deeper inside her as her muscles clenched tightly around him. He came with her, emptying himself into her in powerful thrusts that drove all the breath from her lungs. Falling over him, she trembled from head to toe…completely, one hundred percent in love with him. God.

Cord gathered her up in his arms, and she burrowed in, hiding her face, not ready for him to see. Not now. It would kill her if he saw it and said goodbye. So she lay against him for long moments, hiding, and when she could breathe again, she pressed her mouth to his throat.

He made a sound like a contented purr and stretched, lifting his head and meeting her eyes with his own warm ones. Reaching up, she touched his face, she couldn't help herself. And then it was her turn to practically purr when he rubbed his stubbled jaw against her palm. "Sleep with me," he murmured.

She went still. She'd love nothing more, but she couldn't. Not without giving herself away. "Gotta get up early, I have work—"

"We can do early."

Oh, God. The knot in her belly tightened. "Not this early. In fact, it's really late…" She made a show of lifting her head to find the time. "Yeah, it's three. Gotta get to bed, big guy."

"Lexi."

She absorbed the terrifying gentleness of his tone and let it galvanize her into action. She jumped up and started gathering clothes. Then she turned and bumped right into Cord, nearly knocking him to his ass. "God! I'm sorry!"

He dropped his cane to catch her, and leaned back against the bathroom sink, holding her to him. "Lexi."

"You're naked."

"So are you." He gave her a small smile, something new in his eyes to go with the usual affection and heat. "I think we should talk."

Great. *Now* he wanted to talk. "It's three," she repeated, struggling a little to get free, but the guy was like a brick wall when he wanted to be. "I have to—"

"Barrel out of here, yeah, I know. Just like you barreled into my life when I got back, assuming we were still friends. And goddamn if you haven't barreled your way into the heart I'd forgotten was still whole and beating."

Oh, God. "I didn't mean to—"

"You refused to let me wallow, you refused to let me settle." He smiled. "You took me bodysurfing, Lexi. You took me to scream therapy. Hell, you opened me up to living again, refusing to let me hide behind my secrets. So—" He cupped her face and made her look at him. "What's your secret?"

"Cord." She closed her eyes, then opened them again, shaking her head against the inexplicable panic clogging her throat. She was afraid, afraid of letting her heart open to him any more than it already had. She couldn't lose anyone else, and to make sure she didn't, she couldn't let him all the way in. "I really can't do this now. I have to leave." And this time when she twisted free, he let her do just that.

7

CORD GOT TIRED of lying in bed trying to figure out what the hell had gone wrong with Lexi, so he got up at the crack of dawn and went for a run. Just like old times.

Except, unlike old times, he couldn't run. He couldn't even walk fast. And at the end of the damn parking lot, he had to sit down on the curb and rest.

A car drove by, slammed on its brakes, then backed up. The passenger window rolled down and then he was looking into Lexi's surprised face. "Are you okay?" she asked.

"Perfect."

She sighed. "Get in."

"No."

"Cord."

"Lexi."

She put her car in Park and got out. She sat at his side and studied him for a long moment. "Having a bad morning?"

"You could say that."

"Can I help?" she asked.

"Sure. You can answer a question."

"I don't want to talk about last night."

Too bad. He pulled off her sunglasses and asked the question that had been bugging him. "What do we have, Lexi?"

"Huh?"

"You and me. What is it?"

"Um…a friendship?"

"Is that a question, or a fact?"

She blinked. "What's the matter with you? We're friends. We're…good friends. Best friends, even."

He nodded and looked at the ocean. Then he voiced his deepest, darkest question. "But not more?"

She was quiet a long moment. "I wasn't under the impression that you *did* more."

Hard to argue with that, he supposed. "Things change."

She shrugged.

"Is this because of Brad?"

"No." She shook her head. "I mean I loved him, obviously, and then lost him."

"And your parents?"

He felt her go very still. "Yes," she whispered. "I loved them and lost them, too."

His heart clenched at the look on her face. She was afraid. Afraid of losing anyone else, so afraid she was holding back. "They were older when they adopted you, Lexi," he said gently. "In their fifties. It's not your fault your father died from a stroke and your mother from heart failure the same year."

"I know." She hugged her knees and dropped her head to them. "I know it, I do. I just…" She drew a shuddery breath, and, with a sigh, he wrapped an arm around her and pulled her in.

"You just don't like to risk it," he murmured into her hair.

She was quiet at that.

"I haven't been much of a risk-taker myself since I got home," he told her.

Head still on her knees, she turned just her face to look at him. "I think you're entitled to a break, Cord."

"I've thought about doing as you suggested, you know. I can't go out for the police department, they won't take me because of my hearing loss. But the fire department is looking for arson investigators." Something that actually, surprisingly, interested him. If he couldn't be military, he could still go after bad guys. "Not sure I'm fit enough, though."

"You're strong as hell on the inside," she said. "The rest will come, so you can just get over that fear."

"I will get over myself, since I don't want to sit on my ass the rest of my life. But how about you, Lexi?" He gave her a gentle nudge. "You're still hiding."

"From?"

"Intimacy."

"Are you kidding me?" She stood up and put her hands on her hips, glaring down at him in shock and mutiny. "I beg to differ, seeing we've been about as intimate as two people can get. Just last night, in fact, multiple times."

"Orgasms don't count. Hell, Lexi, you can get those from my showerhead."

She narrowed her eyes to slits as he slowly and, dammit, painfully, rose to his feet. "Intimacy is much more than casual sex," he said. "Intimacy would have been sleeping with me instead of running like a bat out of hell once you were sexually fulfilled. Intimacy would have been waking up together, having breakfast. Intimacy would be—"

"Beyond me!" Breathing hard, she took a step back, eyes bright. "Okay? What you're talking about is beyond me." She pressed a hand to her heart and broke his.

"Lexi," he said softly. "It's not beyond you. We already

have it. It's our friendship, combined with the rest of what comes with a relationship like ours. It's real and binding, and—"

"No. We went into this with our eyes open." She backed away, pointing at him. "*Both* of us. Now you're changing the rules."

"There are no rules. You've never followed a damn rule in your life." He followed her, and ran a hand down her stiff spine. "You're late for work. Just tell me what you want."

She just stared at him, her eyes suspiciously shiny, stubbornly mute.

He sighed and kissed her, a sweet, warm kiss that she pulled back from, shaking her head with what could only be fear on her face. "Stop that," she said shakily.

"Stop what?"

"You just said goodbye to me."

"I think you have that backward," he said quietly.

"Cord." She pressed a hand to her heart again, her other fisted in his shirt. "I don't want to say goodbye."

"Which leads us back to the big question." He covered her hand with his. "What do you really want?"

You. It seemed to be on the tip of her tongue, or maybe that was wishful thinking on his part. Still, he willed her to say it, but she didn't. She said nothing.

In the shattering silence, Cord opened her driver's-side door for her. "You'll figure it out."

And, as she drove out of the lot, he could only hope that was really true.

8

FOR THE NEXT WEEK, Lexi remained stubbornly sure she'd done the right thing by not telling him how she felt.

But deep down she knew she'd been wrong.

She missed him. Things weren't the same. He'd shut her out. He'd even gone to Jacob's for a few days. He'd had a laser procedure done on his leg to lessen the internal scar tissue and muscle damage and his hearing seemed to be better, and he hadn't needed her help.

Hadn't needed her.

She thunked her head down on her table and squeezed her eyes shut. Hell.

It was all her. *What do you really want?* he'd asked. Well, dammit, she wanted so much it terrified her.

It took her a few more days to decide exactly what to do with that knowledge. She brought Cord his mail and he politely thanked her. They had lunch together, but it was strained.

So that evening she took a screwdriver to her showerhead and "broke" it. Then she made lasagna, and when it was ready, she threw together a salad and brought both dishes to his condo.

He opened the door wearing black dress pants and a

black button-down shirt, opened at the neck, tie loosened, sleeves shoved up to his elbows.

He looked edible.

He smiled at her but instead of inviting her in, he leaned on the doorjamb. "Hey."

"Hey. My showerhead's broken. I need to borrow your shower." She lifted the dishes. "I brought a bribe."

"I don't need a bribe to loan you some hot water."

"That's nice of you."

He said nothing to that as she stepped in past him.

"There's fresh towels in the cabinet under the sink," he said when she'd set everything down on the same kitchen counter that he'd had her on, bare-assed, only last week.

She didn't tell him that she'd rather use his towel instead of a fresh one because it would give her a cheap thrill to know the thick terry cloth had been rubbed over his body before hers. "Thanks," she said, and headed down the hall toward his bedroom.

"Do you have plans for my showerhead?"

Her nipples went hard. Bad nipples. Slowly she turned to face him.

"Because if you do," he said, "I'd like to picture it, is all."

"I thought we weren't doing that anymore."

He sent her what could only be described as a wolf smile. "Yes, but I still like to think about it."

Somehow she managed to resist the magic pull of his smile and left the hallway. Even more miraculously, she resisted the showerhead. Good as it was, it couldn't compete with the memory of Cord's fingers and mouth.

When she got out of the water, she toweled dry her wavy hair and left it hanging down her back. She told herself it was for convenience and not because Cord loved it that way.

As they ate, he ran a hand over her hair, then pulled

back as if belatedly remembering that they weren't Naked Friends anymore. She nearly cried. "Why are you all hot and sexy?" she managed to ask, gesturing to his clothes.

He smiled. "Hot?"

Smoking-hot. "You know you are."

He opened a bottle of wine. "Interview. I think it went well."

"Good." She clinked her glass to his and summoned her courage. "To letting go of fears," she said.

His dark eyes held hers. "Yeah?"

"Yeah."

With a warm smile, he drank to that, and when she cleared their dishes she purposely bumped into him at the sink. Reaching out to slip off his tie, she unbuttoned his shirt before he took her wrists in his hands.

"Okay," she murmured throatily, rubbing against him, her wrists trapped, his tie entangled in her fingertips. "You can tie me up this time. But I get to tie you up next time."

He laughed low in his throat, as if he liked the sound of that, but he shook his head. "If we were on naked terms, you'd be so on."

"You'd tie me up?" she asked, intrigued in spite of herself.

"Up, down, any way you wanted it."

Oh, God. "I miss the naked terms," she whispered. "I miss them a lot."

"Me, too."

They moved into each other. Being back in his arms was heaven on earth. He was big and warm and smelled so damn good. She loved the way he held her, his hands rubbing up and down her back, sinking lower to briefly cup her ass before shifting back as if he'd momentarily been unable to help himself.

She stirred against him, moaning at how hard he was. His head dipped, his cheek skimming her temple, his breath soft in her hair. "Lexi."

A warning. He wasn't sure he could resist.

Good. Because she sure as hell couldn't resist him. She pressed her lips against his throat, then nipped the spot.

He sucked in a breath. "Careful. I bite back."

She shivered. "I was hoping you would." Tipping her head up, she kissed him.

He froze a moment, then groaned before drawing her away, holding her by the arms to look into her face.

"Please," she whispered. "I need this, Cord. I need you."

"Why?"

He had every right to ask, and this time she had an answer. The one that had haunted her all week. "Because you were right. I've spent a lot of time being afraid. Afraid of getting too close, of letting anyone in. But that's no way to live, and I never even realized it until you."

"What was it about me?" he asked.

"You make me feel alive." She slid her hands up his arms, feeling the muscles bunch. "So alive. Please, Cord."

With a groan, he dipped his head. "I can't resist you, I don't know why I tried." And he kissed her, hard and demanding, until she wasn't sure of her own name, much less why they'd held back.

She wasn't sure how they got to his bedroom, either, but suddenly she was standing by his bed. He kissed her again, a sound of approval low in his throat when she kissed him back, but when she started to rip off her clothes, he stopped her. He took over the task himself with slow, sure fingers, getting his mouth involved, too, tasting every inch of skin he exposed. Kissing, licking, nibbling. By the time he had her naked, she was writhing in ecstasy on his bed. Then he wedged his shoulders between her thighs, one hand low on her belly holding her down, the other spread wide on an inner thigh, his tongue driving her halfway out of her mind.

"Please," she gasped, sliding her fingers into his hair. "Oh, Cord, please."

"You taste so good." He slipped a finger into her as he slowly sucked her into his mouth.

His words, along with the vibration of his voice, pushed her right over the edge and she burst, the shock waves rocking her body for long moments afterwards. When she blinked her vision clear, he was holding her close and whispering something she couldn't catch. Lifting herself up, she pressed him back into the mattress and kissed him, tasting both herself and his own hunger.

"Lexi—"

She kissed his shoulder, his collarbone, his nipple.

He hissed out a breath. "I—"

Whatever he'd planned on saying turned into a groan when she nibbled her way down his fantastic abs, and then hovered over the most beautiful erection she'd ever seen.

He didn't try to talk again. In fact, she was pretty sure he wasn't breathing.

She caressed one hard thigh, then the other, kissing her way along the eighteen-inch scar there, until he quivered beneath her. Wrapping her fingers around him, she drew him into her mouth.

"Lexi!" His hands came up, sliding into her hair, and when she stroked him with her tongue, his hips came off the bed. "Don't stop."

She loved the fact that she'd reduced him to begging the same way he'd done to her, and she settled in to enjoy torturing him some more, but suddenly he hauled her up his body, his fingers digging into her hips like a vise as he buried himself deep with one hard thrust.

They both gasped in tandem pleasure, and emotions hit her hard—need, desire and the sensation of being filled to completion.

She loved him so damn much.

"Cord—"

"Don't move," he grated out.

She ran her hands down his chest and rocked her hips. Swearing, he rolled them, pressing her back into the mattress, coming over top of her, looking deep into her eyes as he held her down. "You never listen."

Her entire body clenched in anticipation as she bent her legs, hugging his hips with her knees. "Cord. *God, Cord.*"

"I know." He kissed her hard as he began to move, his hands flat on the mattress on either side of her, his face low, eyes locked on hers. Her hands were on his chest, his arms, anywhere she could reach, and she could feel his muscles bunching and contracting with his every movement.

"I can't get enough of you," she whispered, and heard his breath catch. She brought his head down to hers for a searing kiss, and in it she could taste promises and hopes and dreams. Arching up into him, she sobbed out his name as he moved within her, so deep within her, faster and harder until they were both gasping for air, on the very edge, and then she was teetering and then falling into bliss. He was right with her, his arms convulsing tightly around her as he shuddered.

When she opened her eyes, he'd tucked her into his side. He was playing with a strand of her hair, looking into her face. His eyes were soft, melted-chocolate pools she could have drowned in. Leaning in, she pressed her mouth to his chest, feeling his heart still pumping hard as she reached up and touched the side of his face.

He rubbed his cheek across her palm. His thumb skimmed just beneath her eyes and came away wet.

She hadn't even realized she was crying.

"Lexi." His voice was husky, rough with emotion.

"I'm sorry. That was…and then this week…" She shook her head. "Did you know my heart hurts when I'm not with you?"

He pressed his forehead to hers. "Same goes. I missed you. I love you, Lexi."

God. Oh, God, she thought maybe her heart was going to swell right out of her chest. "Then why did you shut me out?"

"You needed the time. But time's up, Lexi. Stay with me."

Suddenly she wanted nothing more than to do just that for as many nights as he'd give her. "You mean tonight?"

He came up on an elbow, and his hand stroked the hair from her damp face. "Tonight, yes."

She let out a breath, telling herself she couldn't be disappointed. Not when she'd dragged her feet over this very thing.

He kissed her jaw, the tip of her nose, each eye and then her mouth. "Tonight," he repeated. "And tomorrow. And the next night."

The knot deep inside her loosened. "I love you, Cord. So much."

He took a moment to absorb her words, his eyes revealing exactly how much they meant to him. "Then stay, Lexi."

"For as long as you'll have me." She looked at him and

saw her future, her everything. "Do you have any thoughts on how long that might be?"

"As long as I have a breath in my body. Is that long enough?"

"I think it just might be."

* * * * *

THE PRODIGAL
Rhonda Nelson

For Brady, who will someday make one very lucky
girl a *wonderful* hero.

1

DYING was the kindest thing his father had ever done for him, Major Chase Harrison thought with a bitter chuckle as he tossed back another shot of Jack Daniel's. The amber liquid had a smooth start and a fiery finish, one that settled warmly in his gut and burned away a bit more of the pain with every determined sip.

Sprawled into his father's beloved leather recliner, more funeral food than he could ever hope to eat stashed away in the kitchen, Chase considered the day's events and congratulated himself for getting through the service without literally cracking up at the hypocrisy of it all. He was here out of duty—not respect, not grief. Not any of the traditional feelings that came along with burying a parent. He took another pull directly from the bottle.

Galling as it was, he was here to get away from a career he wasn't altogether certain he could handle anymore. Harsh though it might sound, his father's heart attack and subsequent death had actually given him the reprieve that he'd needed, the break from the constant horrific images from that damned mission near Mosul. *The terrified screams of children, the agonized cries of parents, bloodied little bodies and the pregnant mother...* That was the one he couldn't get out of his head. The one image he simply couldn't erase no matter how hard he tried.

Little comfort, but fellow Rangers Will Forrester and Tanner Crawford hadn't handled the incident any better than he had. Will had already made the decision to leave the military and he suspected Tanner wouldn't be far behind.

Not that he could blame them.

The death of innocent children—whether his unit had been at fault or not—was just too damned hard to handle. One didn't just simply walk away from something like that unscathed. Will had actually had a child die in his arms and Tanner had been near the school when it had been hit.

Though he knew the reason things had gone wrong— bad intel, conscienceless bastard insurgents with no regard for human life—and, logically, he could even accept that he wasn't personally responsible, he couldn't seem to shake the guilt, the horror of what he'd seen.

Did he want to end his career? He didn't think so. He loved the military, the purpose, the way of life. He believed in the greater good. Frankly, his career had saved him from the very man he'd buried today—his father. And in dying, his father had saved him from his career—or at least this part of it.

Though he'd rather be getting his head on straight at an island resort with tanned, barely dressed women and an unlimited supply of alcohol, he had to admit when he'd driven into the city limits of Hickory Grove, Mississippi, he'd felt a pang of homecoming he'd never expected to feel. He'd thought this place would always remind him of his father. He'd expected the familiar trappings of inadequacy and disappointment to descend with a vengeance and had braced himself for them as soon as he'd spotted the town sign.

And yet…nothing.

In fact, the only time he'd felt inadequate or a source of disappointment had come when he'd handed the funeral arrangements off to his father's secretary, Rorie Whitaker—mixed in with the most powerful sexual attraction he'd ever encountered in his life, of all things. Judging from the delicate *Oh* of surprise that had briefly shaped her ripe mouth and the flash of disapproving censure in her bright-blue eyes, she thought he was an ungrateful, callous, heartless bastard.

That description was more in keeping with his father's character than his own, and he'd be damned before he would let her make him regret the decision. What did she know anyway? He chuckled darkly and tipped the bottle back once more. Other than what his father, the great Holland Harrison, had told her?

He'd heard her car power down the drive to the carriage house in the back where she lived a few minutes ago and sincerely hoped that she would keep her extremely attractive little ass back there. He was in no shape to deal with her tonight—he knew his limit when it came to alcohol and had purposely and purposefully passed it several shots ago.

Furthermore, something about the scrappy little brunette made him feel like he was walking across shifting sand—unsettled and off balance. Factor in the inappropriate astro-*freaking*-nomical attraction he felt for her and his potential to self-destruct escalated accordingly.

In short, though he'd like nothing better than to bend her backward over the couch and take her until one of them—or both—went blind, he needed to avoid her like the plague.

A soft knock sounded at the back door. "Chase?"

Shit. Because he was still a Southern gentleman—although

a drunken one—Chase ignored the impulse to tell her to go away and stumbled to the back door, bottle in hand. He nodded at her. "Evening, Rorie. What can I do for you?" *Or to you? Or with you?*

Her gaze drifted from his eyes—heavy-lidded and bloodshot, he would imagine—to the bottle in his grasp and a mulish line replaced the tentative smile that had been on her face. "You're drunk," she said flatly.

His smile widened and he conjured a neglectful gasp. "Where are my manners?" he said, stepping back awkwardly. He gestured to the bottle in his hand. "Want me to pour you a glass?"

"No." She didn't come in, but seemed to be considering something. "This can wait until later. I'll come back tomorrow."

Perversely, though he knew it was dangerous, he didn't want her to leave. He wanted her company. Felt a weird pull toward her, as though he needed her to make himself feel better. "How do you know I won't be drunk then, too?"

"Because that was the last bottle of Jack in your father's liquor cabinet and I'm going to park my car behind yours so that you can't make a run for another." She frowned. "At least, not tonight, anyway."

He studied her thoughtfully, let his gaze drift casually over her small, curvy frame. Lust licked through his veins. "I know that I should be annoyed by your high-handedness, but strangely enough I'm impressed by your fiendish wit." *And even more attracted. How bizarre.*

She crossed her arms over her chest and the smile that slid over her mouth was distinctly chilly. A familiar emotion entered her gaze—disappointment was one he recognized well—and for the briefest second, he was ashamed of himself. "I'm not trying to impress you."

He shrugged, laughed. "Doesn't change the outcome."

She nodded once. "I'll come back tomorrow."

"I'll be busy."

"Being hungover?"

Chase grimaced. "Cleaning out this miserable mausoleum of a house. Why do you think I rented a truck? I've got to haul all this moldy old shit to the dump."

And perversely, he was looking extremely forward to that. This house had never been a home—it had been a museum with his father as curator and himself the indentured servant. Stripping stain, painting trim, refinishing furniture. While other guys had been spending their weekends at the lake trying to get lucky, he'd been holed up here, working his ass off, listening to his father talk ad nauseum about the architecture of this old behemoth and bitch at him when he wasn't appropriately reverent.

Hell, even his mother hadn't been able to stand it. After eighteen years of marriage, she'd simply packed a single bag and walked away, leaving him in the process. *He needs you,* she'd said. He'd never been quite sure what she'd meant by that. Had she meant that his father needed his help to work? Or that she'd needed him in her life less?

Either way, the outcome was the same. Serena Harrison had left in the middle of his sophomore year in high school and had died of cervical cancer before the end of his senior year. Someone had mailed the obituary to his father. Holland hadn't shed a tear, Chase remembered now. He'd just wadded the little piece of paper into a ball and tossed it in the trash, then resumed business as usual.

She looked horrified. "Haul everything to the dump? Are you insane? These are your father's things. Things he's spent a lifetime either collecting or restoring—or both—and you're going to haul them to the dump?"

Interestingly enough, her voice had escalated while her eyes had narrowed into angry little slits. *Strange the things you notice when you're plastered,* Chase thought. She had a tiny little freckle right next to her mouth and a lock of hair had accidentally gotten threaded through her gold hoop earrings. He briefly debated whether or not to untangle it, but given the atmosphere of hostility, he decided against it. He was going to need his hands to get rid of all this shit.

He felt his lips twist bitterly. "Oh, I am well aware of all the effort my father put into gathering and caring for his *things,*" he said, putting particular emphasis on the word. He smiled, baring his teeth. "That's what's going to make tossing it into the trash all the more sweet."

Her expression was a fifty-fifty measure of outrage and disbelief. "You are genuinely horrible," she said, seemingly mystified.

He took another pull from the bottle. "Then the apple doesn't fall far from the tree, now does it?"

"We obviously didn't know the same man," Rorie said, her eyes unexpectedly filling with tears. Of frustration? Or for his father? Either way it made him distinctly uncomfortable. He had very little experience with crying females and had every intention of keeping it that way.

Chase sighed. "Listen, Rorie—"

"No, you listen," she said with a bracing breath. "I didn't want to discuss this now—" she meaningfully eyed the bottle in his hand "—but I don't see that I have any choice. Before you start throwing things out and dismantling a lifetime of your father's hard work, you should read his will first."

"His will?" He hadn't given it the first thought. As Holland's only heir he'd just assumed that everything that was his father's was now his and he could do with it as he pleased. But from the firm angle of her chin and the determined line of her sexy jaw, that wasn't the case. He felt a chill land in his belly and braced himself for it—the ultimate insult, the final fuck-you delivered from the grave. "What of it?" Chase asked her. "Clearly you are in possession of some key knowledge I am not."

She swallowed, lifted her chin once again. "Holland left you the construction company and all of its assets."

He'd hated that company and had never wanted to be a part of it, which had been another bone of contention between the two of them. While his father had been dreaming of adding "and Son" to Holland Harrison Construction, Chase had been dreaming of jump school and Special Forces training. He'd always wanted to be a soldier, and his father had always wanted him to stay home.

Chase had seen the military as a way to get out from underneath Holland's disapproving, autocratic, manipulative thumb and had worked hard to earn an ROTC scholarship. Holland hadn't so much as congratulated him when the news came through. Instead, he'd retreated to his shop, where he'd been painstakingly refurbishing the dining-room table.

Never good enough, Chase thought. Nothing he'd done had *ever* passed muster with Holland Harrison. Eighteen years under the same roof with the man and not once could he ever remember a single word of praise, an approving nod, any gesture that showed his father was pleased with him at all in any way.

He cast a glance around the kitchen—the antique trestle table, the gleaming woodwork and hardwood floors, the old wood cookstove which Holland had converted to gas himself, and he felt a bitter laugh break up in his throat. But he'd sure as hell been proud of this stuff, Chase thought. His things. His treasures. Inanimate objects.

And nothing for his son.

Fully aware that the other shoe was about to drop,

Chase turned to Rorie and arched a brow. "What about the house?"

Her cheeks puffed out as she exhaled mightily and a nervous smile made its way across her lush mouth. "He left it to me."

2

THERE. She'd told him. Aurora—Rorie to those who wanted to keep their teeth—Whitaker breathed a silent sigh of relief.

Surely it was bad form to tell a grieving survivor that the house they'd grown up in was no longer theirs, but with Chase it was easy to forget the rules of propriety.

In more ways than one, unfortunately.

In the first place, he wasn't grieving. He was somber and silent and, at the moment, quite drunk. Furthermore, the gleeful, vindictive look in his coal-black eyes when he'd announced that he was loading everything up and hauling it to the dump was somehow simultaneously the saddest and most horrible thing she'd ever seen.

What on earth had Holland done to him to make him want to lash out this way, Rorie wondered. What could her kind, larger-than-life employer possibly have done to make his son—the one she'd spun romantic notions about in her head thanks to Holland's constant praise—want to retaliate so heinously?

Honestly, Rorie didn't understand it. Though Holland had never had anything but great things to say about his son and all of his accomplishments, Rorie had known things were strained between them simply by virtue of the fact that Chase *never* came home. Holland would ask, of course, and Chase would refuse, then her old friend would immerse himself in another project around the house in an effort to distract himself, she supposed.

It was hard to believe that this hard-hearted guy was the same boy she'd secretly adored from afar when they were in school. That he was the guy she'd spun princess and prom-dress dreams around, the one she'd yearned for with all the passion a teenager could possess. That he was the same one she'd semi-fallen-in-love-with as an adult through the stories Holland had told of him.

Though he'd never known it, Chase Harrison had been her hero…and she'd just discovered he had very tarnished armor.

It was wholly depressing.

But honestly, the fact that he hadn't wanted to arrange a single thing for the funeral should have clued her in to the extent of his animosity toward his father. "You're his secretary," he'd said. "Surely you can handle this."

She could and did, more out of respect than any sense of duty related to her job. Holland had essentially taken her in when she'd come to work at the construction company eight years ago. He'd invented a scholarship program to send her to college, then doubled her salary when she'd gotten her degree.

Virtually orphaned by parents who were too caught up in their own day-to-day struggles to consider her, she had looked upon Holland Harrison as a fairy godfather, and she owed him a debt she knew that she'd never be able to repay.

But that wasn't going to stop her from trying.

And she was starting right now.

The laugh that suddenly bubbled up Chase's throat lacked the remotest hint of humor. "He left you the house?"

She nodded. "And everything in it, with the exception of the things in your room and in his," Rorie clarified.

He tilted the bottle to his mouth and drained it, then grimaced. He laughed again and she wondered if he were on the verge of having some sort of psychotic break. "Come on in," he said, making a grand, sweeping gesture. "It's yours, after all."

"Not until the will is officially probated," she said, stepping cautiously inside.

"A minor detail," he scoffed. He gestured to the table. "Do you mind if I sit down?"

Oh, hell. She rolled her eyes. "Of course not. Don't be ridiculous."

He narrowed his eyes at her. "My father leaves *you* the house that *I* spent the majority of my childhood and teenage years restoring to his exacting standards and you accuse me of being ridiculous?"

She knew that he'd worked on the house because Holland had proudly shown her all of the little things that his son had done. From refinished doors to bits of trim and tile, he would rhapsodize about Chase's talent and lament the fact that, while Chase had the aptitude—a gift, even, according to Holland—he hadn't had the desire.

Furthermore, she knew Holland had exacting standards. Considering she'd been born into a family that didn't possess *any* standards, to her, it had always been one of the most wonderful things about him.

"He said you wouldn't want it," Rorie told him. He'd never told her why and she'd never asked. But she understood now. There was no mistaking the bitterness in Chase's voice.

Chase snorted. "He got that right." He frowned at her through no doubt impaired eyes. "You look familiar."

It was her turn to snort. "I should. We graduated together."

He blinked, astonished. "Really? I don't remember you."

She was neither surprised nor insulted, though a bit disappointed. She'd spun many a fantasy around this man. Nevertheless, they hadn't exactly traveled in the same circles. Chase had been popular, if a bit distant—he'd rarely attended football games or school parties. She'd always chalked that up to his strange mystique—had told herself that it was one of the things she liked about him, that he held himself apart—but wondered about that now.

She'd had a couple of close friends, but had worked too much to maintain what one could call a full social calendar. Somebody had to put food on the table in their ratty little single-wide in the trailer park, and it sure as hell hadn't been her parents. They'd been too busy drinking, fighting or making up to be concerned with trivial things like food.

He stared at her harder, as though by looking at her long enough a memory would surface in his temporarily pickled brain. A prickle of heat slid down the middle of her chest and huddled in her belly button, igniting a flame in a more sensitive part further south. She released an unsteady breath.

He'd always been gorgeous, Rorie thought, but, impossibly, he was even more so now. Hair every bit as black as his eyes was clipped short in a classic military high and tight. His face was lean and hard now, with none of the boyish roundness of his youth, and his jaw was chiseled so perfectly it would make Michelangelo weep. His brows arched dramatically over his equally extraordinary eyes, and if his mouth made her think of rumpled sheets and massage oil, then his smile put her in mind of hot nights and hotter sex.

He simply had that look—that I-am-fully-aware-that-I-can-rock-your-world confidence and, perversely, that self-assurance made him all the more attractive. If that confidence had been polluted with even the smallest hint of arrogance it would have ruined the effect. It wasn't. He was the walking epitome of sex incarnate and, because she'd clearly lost her mind, she found herself imagining her back against this very table and his—

"Wait a minute," he breathed, as though a light had suddenly gone off.

Rorie started guiltily. "What?"

"You worked at the Dip-N-Sip, didn't you?"

She laughed and nodded. "I did," she said.

He smiled at her—genuinely—and the absence of bitterness made a profound difference in the gesture. Her nipples tingled and a wave of pleasure moved through her chest. "I do remember you," he told her. "Your hair was longer then."

Only because she'd never been able to afford to get it properly trimmed. She shot him a pointed look. "So was yours."

He chuckled and ran a hand over the close-cropped locks, inadvertently drawing her attention to the intriguing muscle play in his upper arms. *Wow. Yum.*

"How long have you worked for my father?" he asked.

"Eight years."

"Since we graduated?"

"Yep." She smiled, remembering. "He was a regular at the Dip-N-Sip and offered me a job. Said that I had a good work ethic for someone so young and that I had potential."

She'd had teachers express the same sentiment, but, coming from Holland, for some reason, it had meant more.

"And you've lived out back in the carriage house since?" he asked leadingly.

"Since the year after I started to work for him. I helped him renovate it."

It had been a dream come true. She used to drive down this street with its grand old homes and dream of living in one of these houses. She wouldn't have cared which— any one of them would have been an improvement over the trailer park. She'd imagined the gilded lives of those who'd lived here—an unlimited supply of hot water, a fully stocked pantry, a canopied bed. She'd always wanted a canopied bed. For some reason it had become the ultimate status symbol in her mind.

She'd laughingly mentioned it to Holland one evening when they'd been working in her carriage house and the next evening when she'd gotten home, a new bedroom suite—complete with the canopy and linens—had been in her future room. She'd cried and promised to pay him back, to work it off, and he'd insisted that it was a well-deserved gift. Until that moment, no one had ever given her anything. She'd never gotten so much as a Christmas or birthday present from her own parents. Holland had become the father she'd never had and she'd loved him from that moment forward.

"Look, there's no delicate way to ask this, but—"

"No," she said, anticipating his question before he could finish. "We were not lovers. I loved your father and I know that he loved me, but it was a paternal sort of relationship, not romantic." She straightened the salt and pepper shakers. "He dated occasionally," she told him. "But he never brought anyone home."

"The house was his mistress, so I'm sure that would have been weird."

The cynical tone was back, she noted, destroying the uneasy camaraderie. Rorie stood. "I should go," she said.

"Your house," he pointed out. "I can move into the B and B. Or leave altogether, now that I don't have to see to any of this."

She felt her eyes widen. "You can't leave," she said. "You've got to decide what you're going to do with the business. You need to go through your father's things. You—"

He looked strangely panic-stricken, as though the idea of tidying up his father's legacy was somehow terrifying. "Can't you do all of that? I'd pay you, of course."

She could and was going to be out of a job because he would no doubt sell the business. Inheriting the house was amazing, a gift she could hardly fathom, but it was going to be expensive to maintain. The taxes and insurance alone were more than the rent she'd been paying for the carriage house. Not to mention the utility bill, which was positively astronomical to her.

She could handle every bit of this for him, Rorie realized. Chase wasn't the least inclined to iron out the details of his father's life, to fulfill his last wishes stated in his will. But Holland had wanted Chase to take care of things, as a son should.

She shook her head.

Furthermore, she thought he needed to do this. No one needed closure more than Chase Harrison, she thought, irrationally convinced of this insight.

"I'll help you, of course," she told him. "But this is something that you're going to have to take care of yourself." She laid her hand atop his and determinedly ignored the jolt of awareness that bolted through her. Her bones felt as if they were melting from that mere touch. Want and longing twined through her. "It's what your father wanted."

Chase sighed tiredly. "And God forbid he doesn't get what he wants, eh?" He looked heavenward. "Pulling strings from the grave, old man? Good one. I'm impressed."

"You should go to bed."

His gaze slid from one end of her body to the other and the playful smile that curled his lips made her heart kick into an oh-hell rhythm. "You offering to tuck me in, Rorie?"

She chuckled softly and backed toward the door. To her chagrin, he got up and followed her…and she liked it. "I don't think so."

"Drink with me and you won't think at all," he said, purposely invading her space. He smelled like lilies and musk, a weird combination. He'd stripped off his shirt and tie, and was clad only in a white T-shirt and pleated suit pants. She could see every muscle beneath the thin cotton, every plane of his abdomen. "I highly recommend it."

Her nipples pearled and her breath suddenly didn't want to go into or exit her lungs. "Good night, Chase," she said firmly, putting a single finger against his chest to prevent him from coming any closer.

"I'll let you take advantage of me," he teased, black eyes twinkling, his voice husky.

Oh, she'd just bet he would. Booze and sex, the ultimate cure-all. He was hurting, Rorie suddenly realized. Because of his father's death? Unresolved issues? Or was it something else?

She didn't know, but for Holland's sake, she would have to try and find out. And, because she was a sucker for a sad case, she would have to help him if she could.

Unable to help herself, she bent forward and pressed

a kiss on his cheek. "I'll see you in the morning, Chase."
The unexpected display of affection momentarily startled
him, giving her the opportunity to duck out of his embrace
and escape.

And that's exactly what it felt like—an escape. But
something told her that this was only a temporary victory,
that she couldn't evade the inevitable.

I'll let you take advantage of me.

She shivered. The same could be said of her.

3

CHASE AWOKE the following morning with a headache of mammoth proportions and a vague sense of unease that rapidly became an enlarged balloon of dread. When the memories of the night before became sharp enough to pop it, the shame set in.

He'd hit on her.

Immediately following his father's funeral.

Right after asking if they'd been lovers.

Smooth, Chase, he thought, wincing with regret. *You really have a way with the ladies.*

Too much alcohol in too small a time had no doubt been a very bad idea, but last night—or yesterday afternoon, more specifically—he'd needed something, anything, to dull the emotion. To quiet the noise in his head.

In the hard light of day, he realized he'd been a coldhearted, selfish bastard. Regardless of how his father had treated him, he seemed to have genuinely cared about Rorie—he'd left her the house, after all—and that affection was reciprocated.

Furthermore, though it was completely self-serving, he couldn't afford to piss her off. He *did* need her help. He hadn't set foot in Harrison Construction since the day he'd told his father that he'd gotten the ROTC scholarship and his father had merely nodded, then gone about his business as usual. He'd only been to the house twice and both of those visits had coincided with funerals—his paternal grandparents. They'd died within six months of each other the year after he'd graduated.

He could find all the pertinent paperwork and had a general idea of what needed to be done for the business, but otherwise he was completely uninformed of his father's life. Rorie definitely had the advantage there and the sooner he was finished with all of this, the sooner he could walk away. Back to the military, for sure. But permanently? He still didn't know. He couldn't imagine another life, another career. He was a soldier.

But knowing it and believing it were two entirely different things.

Though he'd been up since dawn, Chase waited until eight o'clock to knock on her door. He'd brought a couple of ham-and-cheese biscuits someone had brought over yesterday as a peace offering and hoped that she would provide the coffee. He desperately needed the caffeine.

Pillow creases still on her cheeks, a serious case of bedhead and her body covered in a worn chenille robe, Rorie finally opened the door. Her blue eyes widened in guarded surprise when she saw him standing there.

He lifted the tray and smiled, feeling a strange sort of release at seeing her—as though he could breathe properly now. Rattled, he shook the bizarre sensation off. "Breakfast?"

"What time is it?" Her voice was husky and clogged with sleep. Sexy. Another bolt of desire shot through him.

"Eight. Don't you have to be at the office by nine?"

Rubbing her face wearily, she opened the door wider and gestured for him to come in. "I do."

"I thought you would be up already." Though he had to admit, this sleepy, sexy version of her worked just fine. Damn. The way the worn fabric draped over her ass was simply criminal. And the bed-head? Strangely attractive as well. Put him in mind of sex. The hot, depraved variety. His dick stirred just looking at her and he had the almost overwhelming urge to lick the side of her graceful neck.

"My clock would have gone off in fifteen minutes."

"Do you want me to come back?"

Her face squinched up. "Why are you here?"

So she wasn't a morning person. For reasons which escaped him, he found this utterly adorable. "I wanted to apologize for last night."

She looked at him then, truly looked at him, and the floor seemed to shift beneath his feet. Her eyes weren't just blue—they were aqua. Clear, heavily lashed and intelligent. "For being drunk?"

He smiled, chagrined. "And everything that it implies."

She shrugged. "You were entitled. You'd just buried your father."

She made it sound so simple, as though that were the only reason he hadn't wanted to be in his own head. A snapshot of horror filled his mind, *the pregnant woman, clutching her bleeding belly...*

She snagged a biscuit off the tray, thankfully distracting him. "Would you like a cup of tea?"

Not his preference, but he'd take his caffeine where he could get it. "Sure."

She headed toward the kitchen. "I'll put the kettle on. Make yourself comfortable."

Taking the opportunity to regroup and check out her space, Chase set the tray down on the coffee table and settled cautiously onto the couch. It was covered in some ghastly floral brocade that instantly put him on edge and made him afraid of getting it dirty. In fact, the room was packed full of flowers—fresh, fabric and painted. Little vases filled with daisies lined the mantel and a painting of this very house hung on the opposite wall. A large rug with cabbage roses lay against the floor. Needlepoint pillows—more flowers—sat against the chair backs and at either end of the sofa.

It was a veritable garden.

No pictures of people, Chase noted. Not a single personal photograph. How strange. Didn't she have any family? Parents? Siblings? Friends?

Something small and furry attacked his shoes, startling the hell out of him.

"Daisy," she chided, laughing softly as she came back into the room. He recognized the tea set—it had belonged to his mother. "Sorry about that," she said, as the kitten continued to bat at his shoelaces. "She's still a baby."

He reached down to rub the little tabby between the brows.

"She's pretty."

"She's a handful," Rorie said indulgently. "But she's good company. Your father got her for me a couple of weeks ago."

He'd always begged for a pet, but had never been allowed to have one. Wait. Not true. Holland had permitted, albeit reluctantly, his turtle, Skip.

The cat had considerably more personality.

Trying to keep the bitter tone out of his voice, Chase took a sip of tea and then addressed the business at hand. "I thought I'd come with you to the office this morning. Start there and get things sorted."

She added a teaspoon of sugar to her tea. "Shouldn't you meet with Hank first?"

Hank was his father's attorney. Come to think of it, he'd mentioned dropping by his office today, but Chase had been too preoccupied to give it any thought at the time.

"Er...yeah, I guess," he said, dreading it. Hank and his father had been friends for years. No doubt Hank knew exactly what his father had thought of him, the disappointment he'd been. Rorie, too, for that matter, and somehow her knowing was worse. Geez, God, the sooner he was finished with this the better.

Rorie bent down and stroked the cat's fur, inadvertently exposing the side of her breast in the process. His mouth actually watered.

"He says your father left a few instructions on how he wanted things handled," Rorie said.

His mood blackened once more and he felt his lips twist into the familiar sardonic grin. "Of course. He would."

Her gaze found his and the pity he saw there absolutely cut him to the quick. Pity? *Pity?*

Oh, hell, no.

"So did Hank tell you about the house or had my dad?" Chase asked.

She swallowed. "Hank told me," she said. "He wanted me to know before you—"

"—came in and razed the place, I imagine," he finished, trying unsuccessfully to quell the irritation rapidly pushing through his veins.

"That was not his concern," she said, her eyes flashing. "He was afraid that you'd want to come in and immediately sell. He wanted me to know that I would still have a home, since I wouldn't have a job."

His conscience pricked. His father's death was affecting her life much more directly than his own. After all, once everything was settled, he could walk right back into the life he'd left behind. Minus both parents now, which he would admit was mildly disconcerting. No siblings, no grandparents, no parents. He was essentially an orphan, but considering he'd purposely made himself one years ago, he was pretty well-equipped to deal with it.

Rorie was not and he had an obligation, as Holland's son, to see this through. He would treat it like a mission, Chase decided. Would tackle it with methodical precision, one step at a time.

"I'm sorry about the job, Rorie, but I am going to sell the business," he said, making an attempt to keep his voice level and kind. "Not out of spite, as you might think, but out of feasibility." He took a sip of tea and was surprised when he liked it. His mother used to drink tea. He hadn't thought of that in years. "I can't run the construction company from Iraq."

Her lips twisted, but the smile was more knowing than bitter. "You wouldn't keep the business even if you weren't in Iraq. Holland always said you hated it."

"I had no interest in it," he corrected. "Building, fixing and restoration was his passion. Being a soldier was mine." He looked away. "He could never understand the difference and made absolutely no effort to try. It had to be his way, always."

"He just wanted you here. You were his only family."

He chuckled and shook his head. "I was his only whipping boy."

She studied him thoughtfully. "You don't believe that. You have to know that he loved you."

"Inasmuch as he was capable, which was damned little," Chase said with a strained smile. He stood. He didn't like the direction this conversation was taking. He'd buried his father yesterday and that meant burying the past and any feelings about it with him.

Rorie was looking at Holland Harrison through hero-glasses and, though Chase knew the truth, he figured she needed to cling to that image more than she needed to have an accurate account of his father. He made his way to the door, then turned back to look at her. Her mouth was turned down in a sad line and the pity was back in her eyes, making him want to punch something. Or replace the sentiment with a more productive one, like desire. "I'm going to see Hank. I'll be by the office later."

"I'll arrange for the crews to finish current projects, then you'll need to decide what to do about the future work."

"Let me talk to Hank first."

She nodded. "I'll help you however I can," she said, and, for whatever reason, he got the distinct impression that there was a double meaning to her words.

"I'll make it worth your while. I've only got to the end of the week to get everything settled."

Something shifted behind her eyes. Regret? "Then you return to Iraq?"

He nodded, suddenly certain of his path. He'd needed this break—this reality check—but, at the heart of it, after everything was said and done, even after the horror of Mosul, he was a soldier. He cast a glance around her small house, then looked toward the huge Victorian he'd grown up in and knew without a shadow of a doubt that he didn't belong here. This had been his father's path, not his. He sighed. This was Rorie's future now.

The thought was ridiculously unsettling.

4

"WANT A BEER?" Chase offered, extending a long-neck in her direction. They'd been going over the business accounts at his—soon to be her—kitchen table for hours. The small of her back ached and she was getting hungry, but considering the figure he'd quoted for her "help," she had no intention of complaining.

Rorie tsked under her breath, accepting the beverage with a smile. "More alcohol? Do you think that's a good idea?"

"It's a beer, Aurora Rose," he chided, eyes twinkling. "I promise that there will be no repeat of last night."

Rorie felt her jaw sag and lock. "If you value your life, you will never call me that again."

He laughed. "What? Your full name? It's nice. It suits you."

"It does not," she bit out, horrified. She hated her name with a passion. Loathed it. Despised it. Had seriously considered changing it, but had never been quite able to convince herself to go through with it. "It sounds like a friggin' wallpaper pattern. It's Rorie, do you understand? Say it with me. *Rorie.*"

"Sheesh," he said, eyeing her speculatively. "Don't get

your back up, Rorie," he emphasized obligingly. "I was only teasing you."

"I don't like it."

He blinked innocently. "Really? Seriously? I wouldn't have known. I wouldn't have had any idea."

She rolled her eyes, a smile playing around her lips. "Shut up, Chase. How did you find out about it anyway?"

"The will," he said. "Hank gave me a copy."

Ah. "Any surprises? Other than the house, I mean?"

Chase rummaged around in the refrigerator and pulled out assorted casseroles. "Help yourself," he said. He snagged a couple of plates out of the cabinets and found the cutlery. "You can warm it up in the microwave."

"Thanks."

He loaded a spatula with a wedge of lasagna, then a heaping spoon of tuna casserole. "No surprises," he said. "Dad was a micromanager, so everything was in excellent order. Rather than sell the business as a whole, he wants me to liquidate all the assets. We'll finish the work that is already in progress and Hank suggested asking Roger Reynolds to take over everything that was upcoming. He said Rog and Dad frequently covered each other when the need arose." He added a dollop of sweet potato casserole to his plate, making her smile at the bizarre combination.

"What?" he asked, seeing her grin.

She nodded toward his plate and felt her lips twitch. "Interesting choices."

He pulled a shrug. "I don't get a lot of home-cooked meals and I like all of these. Why not eat them together?"

"True," she said, loading her own plate.

He popped the dish in the microwave and set the timer. "Anyway, I called Roger and he said to send him everything—bids and time schedules—and he'd honor them at Dad's estimate."

"Roger's a great guy and he does quality work."

He slid her a look. "He said there's a place for you there, if you're interested. Jeanette's been ready to retire, but hasn't wanted to leave him in the lurch."

Rorie swallowed and felt a gasp of mingled relief and delight rise out of her throat. "Wow. That's fantastic."

Given the current economy, she'd been prepared to ask "Do you want fries with that?" until she could land another office position and was eternally thankful that she wouldn't have to. She'd spent enough of her teenage years in food service to last her a lifetime. Work was work and she was always proud to do it to the best of her ability, but she hadn't spent two years getting her Associate's degree in Business Management to man a cash register.

Honestly, Rorie didn't have huge expectations out of life. She wanted the simple things. Things that other people she knew seemed to take for granted. Steady paychecks, dependable vehicles, central heat and air, a roof over her head, a husband and a couple of kids and enough money to take a moderate vacation every year. She didn't want to be rich, she merely wanted to be comfortable. To be happy. And little things made her happy.

Chase studied her and only stopped when the microwave sounded. "I told him I thought you'd be interested and that you'd be in contact."

He took her plate and began heating it, as well. "Yeah, I am. I'll get everything to him tomorrow. Was he interested in buying any of the equipment?"

Chase nodded. "He's pulling an offer together on all of it."

She swallowed. "That would expedite things nicely, wouldn't it?"

Her plate heated, he set it in front of her and took his seat. "Yes, it would. That gives me a couple of days to sort out the stuff here in the house that I'm allowed to have and I'm done."

She'd been meaning to talk to him about that. Her voice softened. "Chase, you can have anything in this house that you want, whether it's in your designated rooms or not."

His black eyes smoldered at her and his lips curled into a sexy grin. "Anything?"

Butterflies with the souls of killer bees whipped around her belly. If he didn't quit looking at her like that, she was going to be in serious trouble. Between the teenage crush, the adult onset adoration and the unrelenting desire, she was seriously considering letting the chips fall where they may.

And that meant bed.

He was leaving at the end of the week. This was her only chance and she knew it.

"You know what I'm talking about," she said, once again imagining them on this table. *Her legs wrapped around his waist, his bare chest beneath her palms...* She squeezed her eyes tightly shut and fought the warmth pooling at her center. Just one word loaded with innuendo and she was ready. Wet, desperate and willing.

What was it about this guy? Rorie wondered. What made him so damned lethal? What made her want him above all others? Not just physically, though that was potent enough. But she wanted to soothe him, to rub the line from between his brows. She wanted to crawl into his lap and feel his arms settle around her. She'd spent less than twenty-four hours with him and yet she felt as though she'd known him forever. As though her soul somehow recognized his. As though they were tuned in to the same secret frequency and they were the only ones on the air.

And every minute in his company only intensified the sensation. She'd been fighting it—denying it even—all day, but every bit of denial merely crumbled beneath that charmingly sexy grin.

"Th-think about it," she said, struggling to keep her tangled thoughts in focus. "If you decide that you want anything—or all of it—then just let me know. I don't want to keep anything that you would want to have."

His black gaze skimmed over her mouth, lingered, and the tops of her thighs caught fire. "I only want one thing right now," he said, his voice low and slightly rough. A rueful smile shaped his lips and his eyes tangled with hers. "But, unlike last night, I'm not drunk enough to take advantage."

That sounded like a cop-out to her, one that made her curiously frantic to change his mind. "I didn't realize Rangers counted on liquid courage."

His gaze sharpened at the dig and a tiny thrill whipped through her. "You're mistaking courtesy for cowardice."

She slid her full bottle across the table, offering it pointedly to him, then stood and deliberately pulled what was left of the six-pack he'd bought out of the refrigerator, leaned over his shoulder and set it down in front of him. Her breast rested against his arm and the contact made her shiver from the inside out.

It was the boldest thing she'd ever done in her life, but he'd be gone in a couple of days and she'd more than likely never see him again. Desperation made one do things one ordinarily wouldn't do.

And she desperately wanted to do him, so...

Seemingly impressed with her audacity, Chase's eyes twinkled with heat and admiration and a dark, sexy chuckle rumbled up his throat. His gaze never leaving hers, he picked up the longneck and drained it, then turned and stood, towering over her. Heat rolled off him in waves and she found herself leaning forward, instinctively needed that warmth, that closeness.

Then his fingers found her chin and his mouth found her lips and her brain lost its ability to function.

And then nothing else mattered because she was tasting him and the flavor reminded her of…home.

5

HE'D BEEN right.

She had the softest, most wonderful mouth he'd ever tasted. When she'd deliberately handed her bottle to him—that liquid courage she thought he needed—Chase had just about lost his mind. Here he'd been trying to be good, to leave her alone, not to take advantage of her grief and, rather than accept the courtesy for what it was, she thought him a coward? Had she purposely taunted him?

Between the horror outside Mosul, burying a father he'd convinced himself he didn't give a damn about only to learn otherwise, her pitying glances and the perpetual heat buzzing between them, Chase had been an emotional wreck. Factor in the terrifyingly potent need to be with her—just to have her in his sight—and he knew he was treading on shaky ground.

He pushed everything out of the way and put her on top of the kitchen table. No time for a bed—he wouldn't make it that far—and besides, it seemed appropriately fitting.

He was about to feast. On her.

Her greedy mouth fed at his, her hands had burrowed under his shirt and currently worked their way along his spine. He'd had a perpetual hard-on since seeing her in that damned robe this morning and wouldn't have thought that he could want her any more, but he did.

Something about her simply made him *crazy*. She tripped some sort of primeval button inside him, a caveman switch, if you will, and he wanted nothing more than to possess her. To own her. To kiss every inch of her, suckle her breasts and taste her heat, to bury himself inside her and brand her permanently as his.

It was hot and wild and completely out of the realm of his experience, and if he had the least amount of blood left in the head on his shoulders he would have been terrified at the onslaught of feelings—the power of them, specifically—but every bit of energy was focused in the head below his waist and how fast he could get it inside her. He felt as if he was suffocating in his own desire, and if he could just get inside her, he'd be able to breathe.

She ripped the shirt over his head and tossed it aside, then kissed a path down his neck and laved a male nipple.

He shuddered.

Her hands were all over him, slipping and sliding over skin that felt too hot, too sensitive, too ready to do her bidding. He pulled the straps to her sundress down with his teeth, exposing a pair of bare, exquisite breasts, and moaned. "No bra?"

She gently bit his shoulder and worked a hand at the snap of his jeans. Her breath was ragged and low and her fingers were gratifyingly unsteady, as though she needed this just as much as he did.

"It was built into the dress," she explained.

He palmed a plump breast, admired a rosy nipple before taking it into his mouth. "Brilliant design. I think all of your clothes should be made like this."

Her mouth opened in a silent gasp of pleasure. "I'll keep that in mind."

He thumbed the other peak and sucked deep. "You're driving me out of mine."

Her hand slipped beneath his boxers and wrapped around his pulsing shaft, then she worked the slippery skin against her palm. "Hi, Pot. Meet Kettle," she said, laughing. "You think I go around having sex on kitchen tables all the time?"

"Every guy wants to be original, so I would hope not." Nudging her teeny panties aside, he found her hot and wet and ready. He stroked her with his fingers, knuckling the tender nub nestled at the top of her sex while pushing a single finger deep into her tight channel. She fisted around him, squirming against his questing hand. Her back sagged against the table and he quickly looped her legs over his shoulders and replaced his knuckle with his tongue.

Feast, indeed.

Her taste exploded over his tongue and he groaned with pleasure. She was all sweet and womanly and the feel of that soft, soft skin beneath his lips was incredibly arousing. He felt a single bead of moisture leak out of the head of his penis and felt his legs shake beneath him. Rorie's hands were on her breasts and she tweaked her nipples with every lave of his tongue against her swollen clit.

The sight of her touching herself was the single most sexy thing he'd ever seen in his life.

He fumbled around for his wallet, extracted the emergency condom he kept there and quickly rolled it into place. A second later he was nudged up against her folds. The sundress—floral, of course—was hiked up around her thighs and lay in a bunch beneath her breasts. Her aqua eyes were dilated and heavy-lidded and her mouth was plump from his kisses.

Pearled nipples, naked thighs, hot, wet…

He braced himself, pushed in and angled deep. He took

the gasping breath of a drowning man who'd just tasted air and locked his knees to keep them from giving way.

The sensation, the absolute sheer perfection of the two of them together—him inside her—astounded him. His gaze found her equally astonished one and, in that instant, he felt his future twist, tangle and twine inexplicably with hers.

The shock of that knowledge detonated through him, but he determinedly ignored the blast. He'd think about it later. He withdrew and plunged again, desperation making his knees weak. Right now he just wanted her.

IF ANYONE would have told her she'd be acting like a wanton hussy, having sex with a man she'd known *of* but hadn't really *known* on a kitchen table the day after a very painful funeral, Rorie would have raided their purse for their happy pills and escorted them to rehab posthaste.

She'd always heard that funerals made people more thankful to be alive and therefore more desperate to affirm their own vitality by having sex and, while she could certainly see where that might be true, she knew for a fact that wasn't the reason her legs were wrapped around Chase's waist and she had sweet potato casserole in her hair.

She wanted him with a ferocity—a need—that bordered on the insane. It was powerful and raw and wild and with every push of the long, hard length of him inside of her she could feel that crazy energy building in what she knew was going to be the most powerful orgasm of her life.

And it felt as though it had been a long time coming.

"You make me…want to crawl out…of my own skin, you know that?" he asked her, thrusting so hard she could feel his taut balls slapping against her sensitized flesh.

She laughed, clamped her feminine muscles around him

and wrapped her hands over the perfect globes of his ass. "I…might have…a general idea, yes," she said, panting.

A sizzling tingle built deep in her womb, a bright glow that, like a puff of air against a kindling fire, grew more luminous with every stroke of him deep inside her. He was perfectly proportioned, perfectly sculpted and so achingly, beautifully male that it almost hurt to look at him. *Mine for the moment,* she thought, giving his rear a possessive squeeze. The little movement seemed to give him a thrill and he pushed harder and deeper and harder still.

The old but thankfully sturdy table squeaked in protest and with every thrust she could hear the dishes rattle farther toward the edge, but she didn't care. The only thing that mattered was the feel of him deep inside her, the utter perfection of his skin beneath her mouth, the taste of him against her tongue, the look in his eyes as he pistoned in and out of her, as though he were just as caught up in this mindless insanity of need as she was. Every muscle in his body was tensed and ready, and the breath coming in hard little puffs out of his lungs sent a thrill of feminine pleasure through her.

She was doing this to him. *She* was making him lose it.

The heady thought made that glow burst into a white-hot flame and three strokes later, she screamed and bucked beneath him as the orgasm suddenly crested. He pushed harder, faster, pounding into her. She came to the tune of the dishes shattering on the floor. Her vision blackened around the edges, her lungs refused to work, her mouth opened in a long silent scream and her back literally left the table as the release swept through her, convulsing through her body in wave after wave of wonderful, orgasmic bliss.

She drew her knees back, giving him more access, and she tightened around him while giving his ass another squeeze. He came then, seated himself so firmly in her that she didn't know where he began and she ended and she didn't care. In that instant they were one flesh, united in the sublime perfection of the best orgasm of her life.

His breath came in jagged little puffs and he jerked and pulsed inside of her, setting off little sparklers of pleasure deep inside her womb. Tension melted out of every muscle and the smile that slid over her mouth was absolutely euphoric. She knew she looked like a smitten moron and she didn't care.

She slid a finger up his spine and he drew back to look at her.

"I think that you're going to have to take advantage of me again," Rorie said.

He grinned. "I'm going to need more beer."

She was still breathless, but managed to chuckle. "I'll buy stock in Anheuser-Busch."

His smile faded a bit, turned serious. "I leave in two days."

Rorie understood exactly what he meant. *I'm temporary. This won't last. I can't stay.* And if she'd learned anything from Holland, it was that. Chase would leave. But she was going to get as much of him as she could before that happened and she'd deal with the consequences later.

"Then we'd better not waste any time, huh?"

6

AS A RULE, Chase didn't spend the night in a woman's bed. Though he was a soldier and had been trained to fall asleep when the opportunity existed whatever the circumstances—honest to God, he could doze through a hurricane while wrapped around a light post if necessary—he still nevertheless always knew his exit plan and typically rolled out of bed a few minutes post coital bliss. The implied intimacy of actually spending the night with a woman fostered a false sense of hope for the relationship and therefore he typically abstained.

He hadn't last night.

His gaze drifted to Rorie, who was presently seated on his bed going through a box of his old photographs and school paraphernalia he'd never bothered to get rid of. A soft smile curled her lips and the light from the tall windows spilled over her hair, painting the black locks with a silvery glow.

"You were such a baby," she said, studying an old baseball picture. "Just look at that face. Smooth as a baby's butt."

"I don't know if I like that comparison," Chase muttered,

sending her a dark look while he carefully stacked up old clothes to be given to a local charity.

She sighed. "I always thought you were handsome, you know," she told him matter-of-factly. "You and Richard Chandler. But you were the one I used to dream about going to the prom with."

Irrationally pleased, Chase looked up at her. "Really?"

She laughed. "I had the biggest crush on you," she confessed with a self-conscious chuckle. "And when I went to work for your father, it only got worse. He was always telling me stories about you, how spectacular you were."

Chase felt his expression freeze with surprise. He'd never imagined that his father would ever have had anything nice to say about him. He'd never issued the first pat on the back or paid him the least bit of a compliment.

"He'd show me parts of the house you'd worked on or tell me about your promotions," she continued, unaware of the little bombshell she'd just dropped. She looked up and grinned at him. "You've had the starring role in a lot of my fantasies for years," she confided. "I bet that sounds silly to you, doesn't it?"

Chase grinned. "You just told me that you've had fantasies about me," he said, running the pad of his thumb along her cheek. "And that's not silly in the least. It's damned flattering." He frowned. "Of course, whether or not I've lived up to those fantasies…now, that's another kettle of fish altogether."

She laughed and the sound made something near his heart shift. Affection welled in his chest as he stared at her and he suddenly realized her answer was much more important than he'd realized. "Oh, you have more than lived up to them, I can assure you." She sighed. "Numerous times, as you well know."

Chase grinned, unaccountably relieved. And he did know.

Last night on the kitchen table, then again just after midnight in her canopied bed—the one his father had actually bought for her, she'd confided—and again this morning, in the shower they'd taken together. He couldn't get enough of her. Couldn't seem to slake his lust, to take the edge off. It was slightly terrifying, particularly considering he was leaving bright and early the day after tomorrow. This explosive relationship would come to an abrupt end, would finish just as quickly as it had flared. The thought left him unreasonably depressed.

Chase told himself that he'd met her at a vulnerable point in his life, at a crossroads between tragedies—Mosul and the death of his father. He told himself that he was clinging to her because of the sex and the sex was phenomenal because of the extraordinary circumstances.

And he was hoping if he kept telling himself this, at some point he'd start believing it.

He grinned at her and felt masculine satisfaction swell in his chest. "I aim to please."

"And hit the bull's-eye every time."

He shrugged. "What's the point otherwise?"

"Exactly, but from past experience I can tell you that not all men are as concerned with hitting the mark as you are."

Though he knew she wasn't a virgin, the idea of another man touching her made a red haze swim before his eyes and a nauseous feeling swirl unhappily in his gut.

"Oh?" he asked, fishing, of course.

She looked up, seemingly realizing that she'd said too much. "Not a lot of experience," she qualified. "I was a late bloomer and didn't have a lot of time for… Well, I just didn't have the time to invest in relationships. I dated Shane Compton for a while. Do you remember him?"

Chase nodded, his jaw hardening. "Vaguely."

"We were very briefly engaged."

He pictured her in a white gown and felt something strange shift around in his chest. He'd never imagined a lover in a white gown. Not once and, while he was firmly rooted in denial, he wasn't so stupid that he didn't recognize the significance. "How briefly?"

A rueful smile drifted over her lips and she tossed another picture back into the box. "Long enough for him to convince me not to wait for the honeymoon, then he called everything off."

"Bastard."

"Slimy, miserable, rotten lying bastard," she corrected, making him smile. "But it was my own fault for being stupid. I knew better. I just had wanted to wait. My parents hadn't and I wasn't what you would call a happy surprise. I was a we-have-to-get-married baby and I don't think either of them ever truly forgave me for that."

He felt his fingers tighten around a T-shirt and was surprised at the level of violence he suddenly wanted to deliver on her behalf. "Bitch and bastard respectively, then."

"I agree."

No wonder his father had done so much for her, had essentially taken her in. She hadn't had anyone. He knew she'd always been working at the Dip-N-Sip when he'd gone in. Clearly that had been out of necessity. She'd already mentioned that she'd grown up in Piney Acres, a run-down little trailer park on the bad side of town.

"Do you see them much? Your parents, I mean?"

She shook her head. "Not if I can help it. All they

ever want is money, so I try to avoid them as much as possible."

He felt his shoulders sag. "That sucks, Rorie."

"That's why your dad was so special to me, Chase." She looked up and her bright blue eyes caught his. She cocked her head. "I know he wasn't your favorite person, but he was good to me. In a lot of ways, he saved me."

"You would have saved yourself."

"True," she admitted. "But it would have taken me a lot longer than it did. Your dad gave me a job and put me through school. Did I tell you that?" she asked, referring to the latter, he assumed.

"That he'd sent you to college? No," he admitted.

"He did." She looked around the room and released a little sigh. "It's funny, though, you know? You grew up here in this beautiful house and saw nothing but a pile of old boards and hard work. I grew up in a crappy single-wide and dreamed of living in a house like this." She laughed softly. "I thought if I had great home I wouldn't have any problems. I guess anywhere can be a prison if it's somewhere you don't want to be, eh?"

Chase silently agreed. Unsettled, he opened another drawer and started pulling things out. "It wasn't so much the house as it was Holland," he finally told her, not altogether sure of why he felt compelled to share that little bit of insight with her.

"Oh?" she said, using his own ploy against him.

He grinned, letting her know that he hadn't missed it, and she smiled in return. He felt that peculiar sensation in his chest again and quelled the panic that suddenly set in.

Easy, boy. It's nerves. It's the sex. It's the circumstances. Nothing to freak out over.

"Yeah," he said. "I'm glad he was good to you, Rorie,

I really am." He winced. "But he made my life a living hell."

She made a sympathetic sound. "I'm sorry."

"You shouldn't be. He was the one who owed me an apology." And he'd never get it now, Chase realized. Things would never be resolved. He would never get the pat on the back, the I'm-proud-of-you-son moment he'd secretly yearned for most of his life. The opportunity was past.

"He was that terrible, then?"

"He was horrible. Nothing—*nothing*—was ever good enough. Do you have any idea how many times I refinished the spindles on the staircase? How many times I stripped, sanded and restained each and every one of those difficult little things? *Dozens,*" he told her. "Over and over and over again. 'Surely you can do better than that, Chase,'" he mimicked his father. "'You missed a spot here, son. Start over.'" He laughed bitterly. "And he meant it. There was no repairing one little bad spot—it was redo the whole damned thing. Every time." Another disbelieving chuckle rumbled from his chest. "Every freaking time."

"We did refurbish the carriage house together, so I do have a general idea of what you're talking about." She frowned. "Though he must have learned his lesson from you because he would catch himself criticizing and would stop and tell me I was doing fine." She laughed. "And, of course, if he was being unreasonable, I'd simply tell him he was full of shit."

Chase felt his eyes widen and he choked on a shocked laugh. "You didn't."

She laughed. "Oh, yes, I did. Don't get me wrong, I was grateful, but I wasn't going to let him bully me. I was not a perfectionist and if that's what he was looking for, then he would have to do it himself." She chuckled and her gaze turned inward. "He was shocked at first—I don't guess anyone had ever had the nerve to argue with him before—but he just laughed it off and told me I had moxie."

Chase shook his head. "I don't think he would have laughed it off if I'd told him he was full of shit."

She chewed the inside of her cheek and her eyes twinkled with humor. "Probably not. You were his son, after all. I wasn't and therefore probably got away with a lot of things you didn't." She paused. "But he always bragged about you, you know. Said you had a better hand than seasoned carpenters and had an eye for detail that was unmatched."

Shock detonated through him once again and he tried to play it off by lobbing a pair of old socks into the wastebasket. He cleared his throat. "Really? Wow. He, uh…" He laughed uneasily. "He never mentioned anything like that to me."

"That's too bad," she said, as though she hadn't just punched a hole through his gut with her offhand account. "It would have been better coming from him."

True, Chase thought, his throat working with the effort to stay clear. Emotion he'd denied and hadn't wanted to deal with reared up and threatened to take him down.

He was afraid he wouldn't resurface.

Rather than deal with it—feel it—he launched himself at Rorie, tackling her against the bed. The breath whooshed out of her lungs and she squealed with delight as his lips found her neck.

"I thought we weren't going to do this until after we'd gotten your room finished."

"Change of plans." He unbuttoned her shirt and buried his nose in her cleavage.

"No beer first?"

"You talk too much."

She flexed her hips up against him and her hot little

hands tugged his shirt from his jeans. "Then you should probably find a better way to occupy my mouth."

Smiling, he kissed her again. "I aim to please."

7

"THE INNER SANCTUM," Chase breathed, stepping into his father's room the next day.

"I've never been in here, either," Rorie said. "Just walked by and caught a glimpse through the open door."

Holland had had a canopied bed, as well, only his was much more grand and masculine. The top was wide, heavily carved and draped with red velvet. The wood—mahogany, she thought—was dark and topped with marble. Wool rugs painted the floor and vintage Audubon prints hung on the walls. The room smelled of orange furniture polish and Old Spice and her eyes inexplicably filled with tears.

She missed her friend.

"Hey, hey, hey," Chase said, wrapping her in a hug. She must have sniffled and given herself away. "It's all right, Rorie."

She swallowed thickly. "It will be, I know. I just miss him."

Predictably, as soon as the conversation turned to anything remotely close to emotional territory, Chase kissed her. And that kiss almost always turned into something much more substantial. She knew he was into her, knew that he enjoyed the sex as much as she did—and that was *a lot*—but this determination simply to not think about the tough things by substituting thought for action wasn't healthy.

Unfortunately, he was leaving in the morning and she didn't have the willpower or the wherewithal to tell him that.

Because, God help her, she wanted him just as much.

Though it took every bit of strength she possessed, she slowly ended the kiss. "We'd better get to work," she reminded him. "I have plans for you this evening, so we've got to stick to the timeline."

He nodded regretfully. "You're right." He turned to the closet. "All of the clothes can be given to charity, of course," he said. "Let's start there."

They worked in silence for the better part of the morning, carefully bagging up the contents of Holland's closet, which, strangely enough, included a lot of Chase's mother's things. That had thrown him. "He never got rid of this stuff," he said, fingering a silk blouse. "Wow. I just always thought…"

"You thought what?"

His lips twisted. "I thought that he didn't care that she'd left and yet he kept her things, almost as if he were hoping she'd come back."

"Come back?" Rorie asked, confused. "I thought she died."

His expression was thoughtful and he continued to stare at the shirt. "She did. But she'd left first. Packed a single bag and walked out on us."

Ahh. Holland had never mentioned that part. He'd just told her that Serena had died. She swallowed, wondering if he'd been too ashamed to tell her that his wife had left him. And not just him, but her son. How could she? How could she have left them? Her gaze drifted to Chase. But it certainly explained a lot.

"He would talk about her occasionally," she told him. "Said she could make the best apple pie he'd ever had in his life and that the first time he'd seen her smile, he knew she was the girl for him."

"I can't believe he didn't get rid of this stuff," Chase muttered. "I watched him wad up her obituary and toss it in the trash. He hadn't batted a lash, hadn't shed the first tear."

"Granted, that's the usual way people express grief, but not everyone is the same." *You take me to bed when you get too close to an emotional meltdown,* she thought but didn't say. Rorie blew out a breath. "He cared, Chase. He just kept everything close to his vest."

"I wish he hadn't," he said. "I always felt weak for caring that she'd walked out on us."

Her head jerked up. "Weak? For caring that your mother left you?" She was appalled. How could he— Why would he—

His mouth curled into that cynical smile. "You live with the ice monster, you take on some of his qualities."

"But he wasn't an ice monster, was he?"

Chase shoved the blouse into the bag. "Not as much as I'd thought," he muttered.

Well, that was progress at least. She started to point out that she'd thought he was cold for not crying at his own father's funeral, but once again bit her tongue. Chase Harrison had absolutely no idea how to express his emotions. He covered pain with a grin and substituted sex for the harder stuff, the things he didn't want to deal with. He was a master at avoiding anything emotionally unpleasant.

And she was relatively certain she was falling in love

with him. Not just the fantasy, not as a byproduct of the crush, but *him*.

And that was going to be especially *emotionally unpleasant* when he left tomorrow morning.

IF FINDING his mother's clothes still waiting for her in the closet had shaken Chase, then discovering the scrapbook of his accomplishments tucked inside his father's bedside drawer rattled him to his foundation. He felt the bed shift as Rorie settled in next to him.

"What have you got there?" She gasped and traced a finger over a newspaper clipping announcing his ROTC scholarship. "Look at you," she breathed. "What's this for?"

He told her, but had to clear his throat twice before he could get the words out. He flipped through the rest of the book, his world shifting with every page.

Every scrap of paper that had ever had his name printed on it was tucked away in this book, Chase realized. Baseball stats, the church bulletin announcing his baptism, his graduation program. They were all there. And pictures. Candids and professional shots, school photos, his first military photo. Little bits of his whole life had been documented there. He turned to the last page and found a wrinkled scrap of newspaper along with a tiny card that said In Memoriam. It was the kind they gave you at the funeral home with the loved one's name printed on one side and the Lord's Prayer on the other.

It was his mother's.

He'd gone.

His throat tightened painfully and the anguish he'd been denying for the past several days suddenly reared up and delivered a heavy blow. Instinctively, he turned to Rorie. He made quick work of her clothes, taking them off or just moving them out of his way. He tasted her nipple and heard her sigh, felt the breath leak out of her lungs. He was desperate to feel her skin against his, her small hands sliding over his body. He needed the oblivion he'd find between her thighs, the grace in her touch.

God help him, he just needed *her.*

A truth he didn't want to examine—like so many others he'd discovered since coming home—lurked in that thought, but he tucked it away and pushed into her.

She drew her legs back, welcoming him in, and immediately the ache in his chest subsided and he could breathe again. The idea of leaving her sent a dart of panic directly into his heart and he channeled the energy of that alarm into another part of his body, pounding into her, branding her, making her his.

Her sweet heat tightened around him and her hands slid possessively over his ass, urging him on. Her pebbled breasts raked against his chest, the soft globes absorbing the force of his thrusts.

Rorie rolled him onto his back, then straddled him. "Let me," she said, sinking onto him, taking the whole of him into her perfect little body. Creamy shoulders, dusky-tipped breasts, a smooth concave belly, the generous flare of her curvy hips, soft dewy curls between her thighs. Her bright eyes were sleepy-looking with desire, her cheeks flushed and the smile that drifted over her plump, carnal mouth… The corner of that grin simply hooked him, Chase realized.

She smiled…and he knew in that instant she was the girl for him.

The orgasm rocketed through him, taking him completely by surprise. He felt his lips peel back from his teeth and he bucked harder beneath her, then bent forward and flattened the crown of her breast against the roof of his mouth. He found the sweet spot at the top of her sex and stroked—once, twice, three times—and she came for him. Purred, shattered, screamed. It was wild and desperate and the sound of satisfaction that tore from her throat as her feminine muscles clamped around him was one he'd never forget.

Breathing heavily, she collapsed against his chest. He stroked the fluted edge of her spine, more content and more complete than he'd ever felt in his life.

"I'm, uh...I'm not real good at expressing my feelings," Chase told her. "But I like you a whole lot."

She drew back and smiled down at him, blue eyes twinkling and sated. "I like you a whole lot, too," she said.

And just like that, he was hers.

"I'M NOT going to wake you up in the morning," Chase told her. They were currently curled up in her bed, naked and tangled around one another.

Rorie swallowed hard. This was always the outcome. She'd known this. "What time do you have to leave?"

"Four."

She glanced at the bedside clock and chuckled weakly. "You mean in three hours, then?"

He winced. "Damn. Yeah, I guess I do."

She knew he was relatively packed. They'd finished cleaning out his father's room and, under the guise of needing to feed the cat, she'd come home to give him a bit of privacy. The desperation in his touch after he'd discovered the scrapbook had absolutely broken her heart and had obviously turned his entire perception of his father on its head. Which was good, Rorie thought.

Chase had needed to know that his father had cared about him, had wanted him back and, while she wished they could have sorted this out before Holland died, at least Chase knew now that his father had loved him, that he had been proud of him.

"Are you sure you don't want the house, Chase?" she asked again, fully prepared to give it up.

"I don't, Rorie. Dad left it to you and I want you to have it." He laughed softly and stroked her upper arm. "It's meant more to you than it ever meant to me."

True, she knew. That house had represented a life that she'd wanted, security and comfort. She loved everything about it. But she would never walk into it again and not be reminded of Chase, of what he'd come to mean to her in so short a time. She wouldn't have believed that it was possible that she could fall so completely for someone in just a few days and yet…she could feel him in her blood, in her bones, in every cell in her body. She'd undergone a chemical change and knew she'd never be the same.

The fantasy had become the reality and so, so much more.

"I'll oversee everything else," she told him, her voice thickening. "Finish up things at the business for you."

He was quiet for a minute and when he spoke, his voice, too, was a bit shaky. "I appreciate it. You've been great," he said. "I'm not good at…saying the things I need to say, but…I couldn't have gotten through this without you."

Her throat swelled.

"I, uh…I was in pretty bad shape before I ever got here," he admitted, confirming some of her suspicions. "To tell you the truth, I was glad when I got the call about Dad. Not because he was dead," he hastened to add. "But because it gave me the opportunity to leave for a bit. It offered an escape."

She frowned and burrowed closer to him. "An escape? From what?"

"From being a soldier and all that implies." He sighed. "Don't get me wrong, I love it. It's what I was born to do. I love the lifestyle, the purpose, the camaraderie. I don't even mind the war," he admitted. "It's the death I'm struggling with."

Ahh. "Unfortunately, they go hand in hand."

"Yeah," he agreed solemnly. His sigh stirred her hair.

"What happened?"

"A lot of complicated nonsense that ultimately took the lives of innocent women and children. The soldiers on both sides know that death is an option, that it can happen. But you sign up anyway, you know? Because you want to do your part. God and country and all that." He paused and she could feel the grief rolling off him. "But the innocent people caught in between…that's where it gets tough. There was this pregnant woman in the midst of all that horror. I can't get her image out of my head. She's with me all the time now."

Her heart broke at the despondency in his tone. It tore at her and ate her up and just imagining the picture his words created made her wince with regret and remorse.

He'd *seen* it.

She hugged him closer. "I'm so sorry, Chase."

He sighed. "It is what it is."

"And yet you still want this life, knowing that something like this could happen again?"

"I want this life because I want to *stop* something like this from happening again," he told her. "Is that unrealistic? Probably. But I can't not try. When we stop trying, we're screwed, you know?"

Honor, she thought. *Antiquated, yes, but still evident. Still out there.* "You're a fine man, Chase Harrison."

And she meant every word.

She felt him smile against her head and he tightened his arms around her. "Thank you. You're pretty damned special yourself."

"Nah," she told him. "I'm just a worker bee. You've got a cause."

"Not true," he scolded. "Your cause is to do the best that you can do, to be better than you were taught. That's noble. That's just."

She smiled, pleased at his assessment. "Well, I guess when you put it like that I don't sound so bad, do I?"

"You're not bad. You're fabulous. I'm…going to miss you."

She was going to miss him, too. Desperately. "We'll have to keep in touch," she said. "This is not a goodbye," she told him. "This is an until later."

His laugh rumbled through her. "An until later," he repeated. "I like that." He kissed her again, slowly, deeply, with a frantic edge she recognized because she felt it herself. "I'd better go," he murmured. "I've got to finish getting my own stuff together and return the rental."

She felt tears prick the backs of her eyes, but was determined not to cry in front of him. "Okay."

He pressed another lingering kiss to her forehead. "Until later," he murmured and slipped quietly from the room.

Then she broke down.

WITH EVERY STEP he took away from her Chase felt as though he were leaving a part of himself behind. He'd never look at another flower and not think of her. He'd never think about his old house again and not wonder which room she was in and what she was doing. He'd made love to her from one end of the old Victorian to the other, had taken her the first time on the kitchen table. He'd confided things in her he hadn't shared with another soul, and leaving her now felt so…wrong, so heinous, it was all he could do to put one foot in front of the other.

He quickly showered and gathered his things, then

loaded them into the car. The bulk of the items he'd decided to keep—mementos, his father's pocket knife, a painting that his mother had loved—were going to be put in storage until he had a proper place to keep them. Rorie had offered to take care of that, as well. She'd offered him everything without expecting a single thing in return.

Extraordinary.

She was one of a kind. She was hardworking, sexy and loyal. She was funny and smart and had a hair-trigger temper he found oddly endearing. She didn't like her food to touch any other food on the plate, and she loved her kitten, even though she'd discovered she was allergic to her. She was the most wonderful, fascinating woman he'd ever met in his life and he could easily see why his father had all but adopted her. Rorie deserved this house and all it implied—home and family, security and love—Chase thought as he strolled back inside to make certain he'd gotten everything.

He admired the spindles he'd worked so hard on, the gleaming floors and woodwork, the copper tiles on the ceiling. The previous owner had painted them, much to Holland's horror, and it had been Chase who'd been charged with stripping and polishing each individual square. If nothing else, he'd learned to be thorough from his father. That giving one hundred percent, your absolute best every time, wasn't always worth the effort, but built character.

He felt a knot well up in his throat and swallowed hard. He could see his father in every aspect of this house and, though he'd hated it growing up, Chase now let all of that anger go and simply absorbed the beauty and reverence in every carefully restored board.

Finding the scrapbook yesterday had been like ripping a scab off an old wound. It had hurt. It had bled. But ultimately, that blood cleansed the gash. His father had loved him. He had been proud of him. And, even though he'd never vocalized anything other than criticism and displeasure, he had cared much more than Chase had ever realized. He'd needed to know that. He'd needed that assurance and, in getting it, however belatedly, he'd forgiven Holland. He'd needed that, as well.

He only wished that they had sorted their differences out under other circumstances, but who was to say that would have even happened? Who was to say that they would have ever had the conversation necessary to clear the air? Chase certainly wouldn't have started that particular talk, and he didn't think his father ever would have either. A firm believer in everything happening for a reason, Chase merely nodded one last goodbye to the old place and silently let himself out.

It was Rorie's house now.

Rorie.

He missed her already and hadn't even made it out of the driveway yet. For one insane instant he considered going back and asking her to wait for him until this tour was up, to give him some time to sort all of this out in his head. Did he love her? Terrifyingly, he thought so. Leaving her couldn't possibly hurt so badly unless she owned a part of him, right?

He looked at the house again, the security he knew she needed, and resisted the impulse to go back to her, though it cost him. He couldn't ask her to give this up for him and he couldn't move back here. He was a soldier. The military was his way of life. He didn't know who else to be. How else to be. He didn't have any idea how to make this work.

"Chase!"

He looked up and saw her running toward him. Hair disheveled, old robe in place, bare feet.

"Woman, where are your shoes?" he demanded. "You'll catch your death."

She hurried up to him and her eyes were wet with tears. "I, um…I gotta tell you something and I don't know that I'll ever get the chance or have the nerve again." She was breathing raggedly, her cheeks flushed.

He slid a finger underneath her jaw and smiled when she shivered at his touch. "What is it, Aurora Rose?"

Her eyes flashed with anger. "Don't call me that."

"I love it," he said simply.

"And I love you," she said, her eyes melting with emotion.

He staggered. "Rorie, I—"

She squeezed her eyes tightly shut. "No, you don't have to say anything and I certainly don't expect anything, but I don't think you've heard those words enough in your life and before you walk out of mine I want you to know that *I* love you." She smiled at him, almost shyly, but determined. "That I think you are freaking fabulous. That I am honored to know you."

She was right. He hadn't heard those words a lot when he was growing up. In fact, he couldn't remember ever hearing them at all once his mother left.

She loved him.

Her breathing still shaky, she managed a smile. "I know it's crazy, that we haven't known each other long enough for this. I've given myself every argument…but my heart just won't listen. I'm in love with you, and I just wanted you to know that before you left."

"Rorie—"

She held up a hand. "You don't have to say anything. I don't expect—"

He placed a finger over her lips and her startled gaze found his. "Would you let me finish, please?"

She nodded contritely.

"I don't want to leave you," he said. "I know that I am supposed to get into this truck and drive away, but I don't want to go. The feeling is so strong it's practically rooted me to the ground. I wish that I could ask you to come with me, to give this up." He gestured to the house. "To sell this place and let me make you a home." He sighed, struggled. "I…love you, too, Rorie. But I can't do that to you. I can't be that selfish."

Her eyes filled with tears and her wobbly smile was the most beautiful thing he'd ever seen. "The only selfish thing you can do is walk away from me without telling me you'll be mine, Chase." Her gaze searched his. "This house is gorgeous and I love it, but without love it's not a home, not a true one anyway. My home is with you." She smiled again. "I just want to be where you are."

His chest expanded to the point he was afraid it would burst. Happiness saturated every cell in his body. "You're sure? You'd give this up for me? You'd follow me around the world? You'd wait for me until my tour is up?"

She looped her arms around his neck and, with a little jump, her legs around his waist. "In a heartbeat."

"And you're sure this is the life you want? That you won't be sorry?"

"I am absolutely certain that you are what I want and if that means following you to the ends of the earth, then I'm game for that, too. I just need to breathe the same air as you."

He knew *exactly* what she meant.

"So this really isn't a goodbye?"

She shook her head and kissed the underside of his jaw. "Definitely not," she said. "This is an until later. And later can't come soon enough to suit me."

"I'll be back," he promised.

She smiled a watery smile. "I'll be waiting."

* * * * *

PACKING HEAT
Karen Foley

For SSGT Matt Nelson, the real hero
behind this story.

Thank you for your service.

1

Anbar Province, Iraq

A BULLET whizzed past Matt Talbot's head. He felt the air
stir near his cheek in the same instant that he heard a dull
thwap against the wall behind him.

Instinctively, he flattened his body against the ruined
wall of what had once been a shepherd's hut and swept the
scope of his rifle along the treeline of a distant orchard.
His vision was hampered by the thick black smoke and
flames spewing from the wreckage of the two Humvees
and the lead supply truck that only minutes ago had been
leading a military convoy through the dangerous region.
Now they lay flipped on their sides, twisted and charred beyond recognition by the rocket-propelled grenades that had
destroyed them. The remaining vehicles in the thirty-truck
convoy had veered off the road in two separate formations
and were taking fire from insurgents on both sides of the
roadway.

The desert sun beat relentlessly on Matt's back, and,
beneath the Kevlar vest and camo jacket, his T-shirt clung
damply to his body. Sweat trickled down his face and into

his eyes. He blinked it away, not taking his gaze from the sniper scope mounted on top of his rifle.

For almost a week he'd lain concealed on a rocky ledge nearly a mile from a remote village where intel said insurgents were planning another attack against the American forces. He and his spotter had slept in fitful shifts, had barely eaten, and only after five days of relentless surveillance—with no sign of any insurgency—had they received word that the intel had been false. They'd been extracted from the region by a special ops contingent and had been traveling back to their operating base when they'd made a detour to provide security to the supply convoy. They'd heard the explosions and had seen the smoke just before they'd reached the scene.

Even now, Matt couldn't believe how completely they'd been duped. The local military, with whom they had spent countless days and weeks training, had provided them with the intel about the insurgents. While they had been focusing their attention on that village, the real enemy had been planning their attack along this lonely stretch of road. Matt didn't know if the false intel had been deliberate or not, but it didn't matter. They'd screwed up, and now American troops were getting killed.

The local military had likely been infiltrated. This didn't come as a surprise, but Matt couldn't help but wonder which of the men was responsible. He'd come to know many of them personally, and the realization that one of them had betrayed the American soldiers—betrayed *him*—made him feel both sick and angry. More than that, he felt hopeless. Were they making a difference? Was *he* making a difference? For every step forward they took, it seemed they took three steps backward.

"Christ, what a mess," muttered the man who crouched next to Matt, peering through a large spotter's scope. "If we'd intercepted the convoy just ten minutes sooner, that could have been our Humvee in the lead."

"Yeah, well, timing is everything," Matt replied. "Just remember to keep your head low. We've only got four days left in this sand trap, and then we're outta here. Try not to screw it up by getting your head blown off, okay?"

Just four more days and then he'd be on his way home, far away from this blistering hellhole where he'd delivered death to the enemy more times than he cared to recall. With fifty-seven confirmed kills over the course of three separate tours, he was well on his way to becoming a legend within the marine scout/sniper community.

But he didn't want to be a legend; he just wanted to go home and pick up the pieces of his life. After twelve years of service to his country, he was ready to put his weapon away. He couldn't remember a time when he didn't want to be a soldier, and he'd enlisted in the military right out of high school. He'd excelled at pretty much everything the U.S. Marine Corps threw at him, but found his real niche lay in his ability to shoot. The military had honed that skill to perfection, but Matt knew that sniping had as much to do with observing and reporting as it had with shooting at a target. He didn't just randomly shoot people; he carefully selected his targets before firing upon them.

He'd never had a problem executing the mission, and he'd never lost any sleep over what he did for a living. He firmly believed that he was saving innocent lives by taking out the enemy before they had an opportunity to do harm. He'd known guys who couldn't kill a target because they'd become too emotionally attached to the subject. Sometimes, after days of observing a person—of watching them eat, breathe and laugh—a sniper might feel an emotional connection to the target and be unable to kill them when the call came.

Matt didn't worry about that happening to him. Just the opposite, in fact. Lately, he'd felt so little emotion about what he did as a sniper that he knew it was time to get out or risk becoming someone he no longer recognized.

He wanted a regular job that didn't require having to put a bullet through someone. He wanted to sleep late on the weekends. He wanted to take his bike for a cruise along the coast and feel the cool Atlantic breeze on his face. He wanted to cook steak tips on the grill and drink a cold beer whenever he liked.

Most of all, he wanted finally to meet the lovely Megan O'Connell. The pretty schoolteacher had been sending him care packages for nearly six months as part of an adopt-a-soldier program at the same school where his mother worked. He'd never even met Megan, but her sweetly poignant letters and photos made him miss home in a way that he never had before. Her detailed descriptions of even the most mundane tasks read like something from a Robert Frost poem, evoking images of life in New England and the small coastal town where he'd grown up.

But it was the personal stuff she shared with him that made him long to get back and meet her. She'd only recently moved to Massachusetts from down east Maine, and despite the upbeat tenor of her letters, her homesickness was a palpable thing. He found himself impatient to get home to ease her loneliness. He wanted to be with Megan more than he'd wanted anything else in a long time. He wanted to spend time with her and show her all the places and things that were special to him. Oh, yeah, he'd been packing some serious heat for Megan O'Connell since she'd first written to him.

Her letters had started out innocently enough. She'd thanked him for his service, and informed him that she and her classroom of fifth graders had adopted him, and was there anything he particularly wanted or needed? He'd thumbed through the handmade cards and notes until he'd found a picture of her standing with the children in her classroom. All he could think was that his own elementary school teachers had never looked like her. And a good thing, too, or he might never have made it beyond sixth grade.

In the six months that they'd been corresponding, he'd called her a half-dozen times. During that first phone call, they'd immediately clicked, and ten minutes had never gone by so fast. There hadn't been any awkward silences, only a sense of frustration that they couldn't talk longer. Through all their letters and conversations, her one consistent message had been to take care of himself, to come home safely. She worried about *him,* a guy she'd never even met. How would she feel if something did happen to him? Would she grieve for him? Lately, she'd been finishing her letters with "P.S. I can't *wait* for you to come home!" Maybe he'd spent too much time in the sun, or maybe he was going soft, but he couldn't prevent his imagination from conjuring sappy images of just how she might greet him. She gave him a whole new reason to come home in one piece.

Three weeks ago, in anticipation of his return to the States, he'd taken a huge chance and asked Megan to meet him at a hotel in California for a weekend. He hoped she hadn't heard the desperation in his voice when he'd made the proposition during a brief phone call; he'd tried to sound nonchalant about it. No pressure, and she could say no and he'd be fine with it.

Which had been a complete lie.

Once he returned to the States, he'd be required to spend at least a couple of weeks with his unit at Camp Pendleton in California, but he knew he couldn't wait that long to finally see her.

To be with her.

To his immense relief, she'd actually agreed to meet him at the luxurious Serafino Hotel in Oceanside, California. The room rate had been astronomical, but Matt didn't give a damn. What else did he have to spend his money on? He wanted to make Megan feel special. Hell, she *was* special, and he was looking forward to getting to know her better. He'd even sleep at the marine base if she didn't want him staying with her. He just knew he couldn't wait until he returned to the east coast to finally meet her. There was a part of him that suspected he shouldn't have such strong feelings for a woman he'd never even met, but he didn't care. He knew they were real.

Now he fixed his eye to the telescopic sight of his rifle and carefully scanned the shadowed orchard on the far side of the convoy. "There," he muttered in satisfaction, spotting movement amongst the trees. "Target," he called quietly.

"Target," replied Ginger, named for his red hair and abundance of freckles. He peered through the large spotter scope he carried. "Sector C from TRP 1, right 50, add 50."

"Roger," Matt replied and repeated the coordinates back to his partner as he adjusted the scope on his sniper rifle.

The sporadic *spit-spit-spit* of machine-gun fire from the deadly battle didn't distract him. Nothing short of a direct hit would break his concentration. All that mattered was the target. Eventually, the insurgent would make an attempt to fire his weapon and when he did, Matt would be waiting. Even the brutally punishing sun that beat down on his back didn't faze him.

"Lone soldier behind the tree, carrying AK-47 in right hand," Ginger said in low voice.

Matt peered through the scope at the man who had

emerged from behind a tree to fix his weapon on a marine who was attempting to drag a wounded comrade to safety.

"Roger. Target identified," Matt confirmed, lining him up in his crosshairs. "He's drawing down on one of our guys."

"Dial 400 on the gun," Ginger directed.

"Roger, 400 on the gun. Gun up!"

"Send it."

With steady hands, Matt deliberately squeezed the trigger at the same instant the target fired his own weapon at the hapless soldier struggling to drag the body of a fellow soldier to safety.

Bam!

Immediately and without looking away from the sighting, Matt chambered another round. Through the telescopic sight, he saw the fine spray of red mist where the target had been, and then there was nothing.

"Center hit," Ginger called, as he followed the bullet's vapor trail. "Stand by."

The high, pitiful wail of a crying child reached him, and Matt blew out a hard breath of annoyance as his fingers flexed around the bolt handle of the rifle. He rolled his shoulders to ease the tension. "Roger, center hit, stand by."

"Confirmed hit. Target destroyed."

"Roger that." Matt swept his scope back to the soldier who had been attempting to rescue his comrade and swore as he saw both soldiers lying motionless on the ground. He closed his eyes briefly in regret, but when he opened them again, he saw the second soldier slowly raise his head and it seemed to Matt that he looked directly at him. He recoiled in surprise.

"Damn. That's a chick!" Even as he watched, the female

soldier glanced down at the front of her uniform and when she pressed a hand against her shoulder, Matt saw blood seep through her fingers. "The bastard hit her."

Matt swept his scope across the immediate area, prepared to cover her if she came under attack again. Despite her injury, she managed to grab the other soldier's flak jacket and doggedly drag him to safety. Only when she had reached the relative shelter of the trucks did Matt pull his gaze away from his scope. He rolled onto his side, swiping a hand across his eyes to ease the strain. The pitiful wailing of the child continued.

"Christ, where the hell is that kid?" he snarled, because as much as he wished otherwise, the persistent crying *did* distract him.

"Ah, damn," Ginger muttered as he inched his head around the edge of the wall to survey the destruction below. "There's a freaking kid in the road, right in the middle of the fucking firefight."

Matt craned his head over the low wall to peek at the dusty road. A swift glance told him that this was no kid; this was a baby, sitting in the dirt about a hundred yards away. Matt used his rifle scope to survey the surrounding area. No freaking way the insurgents would use a child to lure the marines into the open.

Would they?

Matt had seen a lot of twisted things during his three tours in Iraq, but something that sick would definitely take the cake. He swept his scope over the tiny village that lay beyond the battle. A woman stood in the doorway of a small house, her face contorted in fear and grief. Two local men physically restrained her from running to the child.

"Shit." He pushed himself away from the ruined wall and bent low. "Cover me," he called.

"Talbot!" shouted Ginger, and made a grab for Matt, but missed. "We got four days left!"

"It's not my time," Matt flung back. Bent over, he sprinted along the low ridge that paralleled the road, keeping an eye on the crudely dug trench where a dozen or more insurgents still fired at the convoy. They didn't see him until he was almost level with them. One man stood up to take aim at him, but was immediately felled by a single bullet, courtesy of Ginger.

Matt veered sharply as two more insurgents stood up. He'd left the M40 sniper rifle by the wall as it wasn't any good for close combat, so he jerked his M14 from his shoulder and swept the area with a spray of bullets, not waiting to see if he'd hit his targets.

He reached the nearest truck and flung himself behind it, peering through the dust and smoke as he regained his bearings. Two marines lay on their bellies in the dirt beneath the truck, firing toward the orchard, while a third provided cover. When Matt pointed toward the child, the third soldier gave him a thumbs-up and shifted his position to provide additional cover.

Matt made his way along the line of trucks until, finally, nothing stood between himself and the child except forty yards of open, unprotected road. Sitting in the dirt, wearing only a grimy white tunic, was a tiny little girl. Matt guessed her to be no more than two years old.

Slinging his rifle over his shoulder, he made a beeline for the kid. A bullet hit the ground near his feet, sending a spray of dirt and rock upward. He flung up an arm to cover his face, but he didn't stop. Bending low, he scooped the squalling toddler into his arms and then continued his sprint toward the mud hut where the child's mother watched with a mixture of hope and horror on her face.

Reaching the house, he thrust the child into the

outstretched arms of the woman, just as something hit the back of his head with enough force to propel him through the open door of the hut. He did a sliding face-plant along the dirt floor, his body curiously boneless. He was only dimly aware that his helmet had come off and had landed beside him. He watched, detached, as it spun crazily on the hard-packed floor until it came to a stop just inches from his face.

Matt struggled to focus.

Attached to the inside of the helmet with clear packing tape was a photograph of a young woman. She had the kind of clean, blond good looks associated with prep schools and summer sailing lessons. Her skimpy white tank top clung to her curves and outlined an impressive rack. The smile on her face suggested she was well aware of how her nipples thrust against the thin fabric, and that she enjoyed the reaction it caused. Of all the photos that Megan had sent to him, Matt liked this one the best.

He blinked as something warm and wet trickled into his eyes, and his mouth was filled with the metallic taste of blood. Darkness fluttered at the edge of his vision.

He frowned. There was something not quite right about the photo. What was wrong with it? His vision blurred and he squinted hard. Then he saw it; the photo was splattered with blood. His blood.

Ah, damn.

His last thought was that now he'd never get to meet pretty Megan O'Connell. He'd never have the opportunity to see where their relationship might have gone. Then darkness descended and he knew nothing more.

2

THIS HAD TO BE the craziest, most impulsive thing she'd ever done in her entire life. Not just crazy, but off-the-charts nutso. What kind of woman would fly clear across the country to spend a weekend with a guy she'd never even met?

The desperate kind.

The lonely kind.

At least, that's what her friends would say. Which was why she hadn't told them—hadn't told anyone, in fact—about her hare-brained adventure.

Megan O'Connell blew out a hard breath. She knew she was neither desperate nor lonely, but there was something about this particular guy that got her heart rate going and her stomach curling in anticipation just thinking about him.

About being with him.

From the first instant she'd seen the picture of Staff Sergeant Matt Talbot on her boss's computer screen, she'd been hooked. More than hooked; she'd been utterly fascinated.

Megan still recalled the day she had walked into the principal's empty office to leave some paperwork on her desk and had been entranced by the other woman's screen saver. She'd leaned forward to study the image more closely. The guy who smiled back at her could've been the cover model for a military beefcake calendar.

Deeply tanned and mouthwateringly muscled, with biceps that looked as if he hefted Humvees for a living, he'd exuded pure, male sex appeal. He wore nothing but a pair of desert camo pants and boots, and the hint of a tattoo peeked out from under his waistband, riding low on his hipbone. She found herself wanting to see the entire design. He'd cradled a military rifle in his hands with the ease and confidence of a seasoned soldier.

But it was more than just his physical appearance that had captivated her. She'd had relationships with good-looking guys before and knew enough to realize that appearances could sometimes be deceiving. With this guy, it was the expression on his face that had mesmerized Megan. He grinned carelessly into the camera, but Megan sensed that behind the devil-may-care manner was a deadly serious man.

A dangerous man.

"That's my son, Matt, in Iraq."

Megan had jerked upright, face flaming at having been caught ogling the image. She had turned to the principal with a breezy smile and quipped, "Well, if he needs any care packages sent to him, just let me know. With a little bubble wrap and tape, I could be there in a week."

Later, when she'd returned to her classroom of fifth graders, she'd wondered what on earth had made her say something so completely stupid. She'd meant it as a joke, of course. But later that week, the principal had stopped by her classroom after school.

"I've been thinking about what you said, and I think sending care packages to Matt and his platoon is a wonderful idea. You could get your students involved and it would be a great outreach program," she'd said, smiling. "I'm sure Matt would love to hear from you."

And so Megan had enthusiastically started an adopt-a-soldier program. The first box of goodies had been ready to ship just two days later, and tucked in amongst the beef jerky, lip balm, magazines and protein bars had been a single letter addressed to Matt. In it, Megan had told him a little bit about herself. She'd only begun working at the elementary school the year before, having relocated from Maine. She'd been excited about the move, but the truth was that she was still adjusting to living on her own, away from her parents and her three sisters. While she'd developed casual friendships with the other teachers, she didn't have any close friends or confidantes. The prospect of having someone to write to—a stranger who was also far from family and friends—appealed to her.

She'd daydreamed that her letters would cheer him up and provide him comfort. In her imaginings, Matt Talbot hunkered down in a fighting hole, weary from a day of heavy combat. He would sit with his back braced against his rucksack and pull her letters out to reread them, and they would bring a smile to his face. In that first letter, she had included a photo and had provided both her personal e-mail and mailing addresses, just in case he wanted to write back.

His first e-mail had arrived the day he received that care package. The message had been brief, but warm. He told her how much he'd enjoyed receiving her box of goodies, and that he hoped she would send more. They'd begun a correspondence that had lasted nearly six months, and Megan had sent him something—a postcard, a letter, a book, a DVD or a care package—every few days.

Before long, she'd begun to anticipate his letters and

e-mails, and she replayed their infrequent phone conversations over and over again in her head, recalling the timbre of his voice and the way he laughed, low and warm. She'd found him incredibly easy to talk to and even easier to listen to. There was a connection between them that couldn't be denied.

As the weeks passed, their letters had become increasingly personal, and although Megan had initially been afraid of revealing too much about herself, he hadn't seemed to mind. If anything, he'd encouraged her. Megan knew she wasn't imagining the bond she felt with this man. Maybe she shouldn't have such strong emotions for a guy she'd never even met, but if the correspondence and phone calls they'd shared over the past several months had made her realize just one thing, it was that she wanted him.

Badly.

She hadn't been in a physical relationship with anyone for nearly two years—not since she'd moved to Massachusetts—and part of her acknowledged that her body craved sex. She rarely went out on the weekends, and the sole time she'd engaged in a one-night stand, she'd been left feeling so guilt-ridden that she'd promised herself never to repeat the experience. When she wasn't at the elementary school, she spent most of her time driving to Maine to visit her family or just reading and watching movies.

But her desire for Matt went deeper than just a physical longing. At twenty-six, she was ready for a serious relationship, and it seemed that Matt wanted the same thing. They had a lot in common, from their schoolteacher mothers to their love of the ocean, to their dislike of the Yankees and any food containing the word *sprouts*. More than that, he made her laugh.

His last phone call had come just three weeks ago. If she closed her eyes, she could still hear his voice, deep and sexy, laughing as the delay in the overseas connection caused them both to speak at the same time.

"I'm looking forward to seeing you—I mean really *seeing* you when I get home," he'd said, his voice curling warmly through her. "I can't help but wonder if you're as gorgeous in person as you are in your photos."

"What if you're disappointed?" she'd asked, chewing her lip.

He'd laughed, low and husky. "Not a chance. Besides, my mom confirmed it."

Eek! He'd talked to his mother—her boss—about her? How much had he shared?

"Confirmed what?"

"What I already knew, that you're smart *and* beautiful. And I can't wait to get to know you better."

His voice was sincere, lacking any trace of lewdness or sexual suggestion. That had been the clincher for Megan. For the past several months she'd fantasized about having sex with Matt Talbot. There was no doubt in her mind that when they did finally come together, the sex would be off-the-charts sensational, but it had been his quiet sincerity about getting to know her that had sealed the deal.

She hadn't let herself think too much about what he did for a living; couldn't imagine what it must be like to be a sniper. She had to remind herself that the men he shot weren't innocent villagers. They were terrorists, plain and simple. They were armed to the teeth and had only one intent: to kill Americans. If men like Matt weren't there to eliminate them, God only knew how many soldiers would die as a result.

But she did worry that eventually the burden of his actions might be too much for him to bear. Although Matt brushed her concern for him away, she wasn't naive enough to think the job didn't take a huge toll on him, both mentally and physically. She'd told him countless times that he could talk to her about it; he could talk to her about *anything*. But he'd insisted he was fine and she'd had no choice but to accept that. She was just relieved that during the course of three tours he hadn't been injured, or worse.

Now he was finally coming home, but with two weeks of active duty left, he would remain at Camp Pendleton in California until his release date. Megan had been frustrated and disappointed to learn he wouldn't immediately return to the east coast. She didn't want to wait a month to see him. She needed to know if he came even a tiny bit close to the image she'd woven of him in her mind.

When he'd asked her to spend a weekend with him in California, she hadn't hesitated to agree. School would be out for the summer and although she'd hoped to do some traveling, she'd much rather be with Matt. He'd paid for her airfare and now here she was, standing on a private balcony at the lavishly expensive Serafino Hotel, in a palatial suite of rooms overlooking the Pacific Ocean. The sun was dropping on the horizon, turning the skies and the waters below to an iridescent wash of gold, pink and blue. The scene was breathtaking.

And Matt Talbot was late.

Turning away from the sunset, Megan stepped back into the room and glanced for the hundredth time at her watch. He should have been here over an hour ago. He'd said he'd be off duty at six o'clock, and here it was almost seven-thirty. Surely he would have called or left a message with the concierge if he was going to be late.

Wouldn't he?

Not for the first time, Megan wondered if perhaps he'd had a change of heart. Maybe now that he was back in the States, he'd realized he could have any woman he chose. Maybe he'd decided he had better things to do with his time than spend it with her. Or maybe he'd gotten cold feet about spending the weekend with a complete stranger. That she could understand, since her own stomach was a knot of anxiety about the prospect of finally meeting him.

Needing a distraction, she went into the bathroom and closed the door. The soft music piped in from the main living area soothed her frazzled nerves. She rebrushed her teeth, smoothed some lip balm over her mouth and then critically surveyed her appearance in the ornate mirror over the double vanity.

She'd opted for a sleeveless white baby-doll dress that hugged her breasts and floated around her thighs. She'd paired it with a simple necklace of strung shells and pearls, and a pair of strappy sandals. Despite the fact it was still early summer, she'd already acquired a light tan. She knew she looked good, so why did she feel so nervous and self-conscious?

Leaning over the marble vanity, she combed her fingers through her hair, letting it fall in loose waves around her shoulders. Would Matt approve? In his letters, he'd said that he liked her hair when it was down, so that's how she'd worn it. Blowing out a hard breath, she turned and opened the bathroom door, and stopped in her tracks.

A man stood with his back to her in the open doorway of the balcony, silhouetted against the brilliant backdrop of sunset and sea, and for a moment Megan found it hard to breathe.

He was tall and starkly male, with broad shoulders and lean hips. Beneath his T-shirt, the muscles in his arms were clearly evident as he braced his hands on the railing of the balcony. A glance took in his camo pants and boots and the military duffel bag on the floor just inside the door.

For a moment, Megan couldn't move. She just stood

there and drank in the sight of him. He was bigger than she had imagined.

More imposing and masculine.

Then he turned around, and Megan stopped breathing altogether. The photos she'd seen of Matt Talbot hadn't done him justice.

Not even close.

They'd failed to capture the sheer energy that vibrated from him. Her first thought was that the guy could have been cast from bronze, from his golden skin and sun-streaked hair to the powerfully muscled physique evident beneath the T-shirt. Only the stark white bandage over his left ear gave her pause, oddly out of place with the vitality that he radiated. A dark bruise marred his cheekbone, and she took a step closer, intending to ask how he'd been injured.

Then she looked into his eyes and was lost.

They were a shade of sea-green so light and pure that they seemed to glow in his tanned face. In the same instant, Megan realized he wasn't quite the specimen of good health that he'd initially appeared. Up close, she could see faint shadows beneath his eyes, and lines of fatigue were etched on either side of his mouth. Clearly, he was exhausted.

He watched her now with an intensity that caused Megan's stomach to do an odd flip-flop, and her heart exploded into a frenzied rhythm.

"I didn't hear you come in," she said inanely, feeling foolish. She'd rehearsed this moment in her head so many times, yet the best she could do was stand there and stare stupidly at him.

"Yeah," he said, his gaze so unwavering that her knees began to tremble. "I knocked, but I guess you were in the bathroom. I used my room key to get in."

His voice was deep and warm, sliding over her senses.

Then he smiled and Megan's stomach did a slow, inverted roll and her equilibrium shifted. She reached out a hand to steady herself. In an instant he was there beside her with a hand at her elbow.

"Hey, you okay?"

Megan refocused and found herself staring directly into his eyes and realized they really were a clear, unsullied green, the same shade as the pale beach glass she'd collected as a child. His pupils seemed suspended in the brilliance of his irises, and Megan shivered as he swept his gaze over her.

"You have beautiful eyes," she blurted.

He laughed softly, a warm, husky sound that washed over her and seeped into her skin, making her long to hear more. Her own physical response to Matt alarmed her. She'd fallen for him based on his letters and their infrequent telephone conversations, and while she'd known he was good-looking, she hadn't counted on the overwhelming attraction she now felt. Everything about the guy appealed to her, from the expression in his eyes to the warm timbre of his voice, to the raw masculinity that oozed from every pore of his body. She'd never had such an irresistible desire to touch anyone the way she wanted to touch him, and she fisted her hands at her sides to keep from acting on the impulse.

"What did you do to your head?" She spoke quickly to hide her nervousness, and her voice sounded high and breathless, even to her own ears. Could he tell she was a bundle of nerves? She cleared her throat and strove for a normal tone. "Are you okay?"

Reaching up, he briefly touched the bandage. "Yeah, I'm good. I got lucky."

Megan didn't miss how his eyes darkened in recollection. "What happened?"

"I took a hit to the back of my helmet." As if unable to help himself, he reached out and stroked a finger along the skin of her arm, seemingly mesmerized by the texture. "But I'm okay now."

Megan stared at him in horror. "What do you mean— you got hit in the back of the head?"

He looked at her, and a muscle worked in his cheek. "A bullet hit the back of my helmet, but was deflected by the armored shell. It penetrated just above my ear. Thankfully, it was mostly spent. It grazed the side of my head, but didn't do any real damage." He laughed softly. "Except for a bitch of a headache that lasted three days."

Megan knew she was staring at him in horror, but she couldn't help herself. "When did this happen?"

"Four days before we left Iraq." He tipped his head down and searched her eyes, and Megan saw the amusement fade into concern. "Hey, I'm okay. It wasn't my time."

Still, Megan couldn't dispel the image she had in her head of Matt, lying facedown on the ground with a hole in the back of his helmet and a growing pool of blood beneath his head. Impulsively, she threw her arms around him.

"I'm so glad you're safe," she whispered into his ear. "I'm so glad you're here."

Matt's arms came around her, and nothing had ever felt so wonderful to Megan. He smelled good, like soap and something minty. She breathed in his scent, savoring the feel of him, still a little in awe that he was really there, with her. Her arms tightened around him and she buried her face against his neck.

They stood that way for several long moments, until Megan slowly became aware that they were pressed together from shoulders to knees. Her arms were wound around his neck and her fingers clung to the strong contours of his shoulders. Her breasts were crushed against him, and his hands were stroking along her spine. His breathing had changed and Megan felt the unmistakable thrust of his arousal against her abdomen. The awareness caused her nipples to contract and heat to build low in her womb.

She pulled away, unable to meet his eyes. "Sorry," she mumbled, smoothing her skirt.

"For what?" His voice sounded gravelly.

Megan swallowed hard and glanced at him. "For throwing myself at you like that." She gestured helplessly, her stomach a mass of knotted anxiety. "I'm just so glad that you're okay."

He scrubbed a hand over his hair. "Oh, man," he said on a half laugh, half groan. "You are making this very hard for me, Megan O'Connell."

"Making what hard?" she asked innocently, but was helpless to prevent a downward glance at the front of his camo pants.

To her dismay, a flush of ruddy color turned his neck and ears red. He drew in a swift breath and caught her gaze with his own, his expression turned serious. "I've waited six months for this moment. Toward the end of my tour, all I could think about was that I'd finally get to meet you, and my plan was just to take it slow and get to know you better, see how things went. But now that I'm here, I can't quite get my head around it, you know?" He seemed a little dazed. "You're even more freaking gorgeous in person. So what I want to know is, what are you doing here with me?"

Megan stared at him, realizing that he was as uncertain and apprehensive as she was. He wanted to go slow! To get to know her better. Megan felt a rush of pleasure at his words, even as she acknowledged that going slow was suddenly the last thing she wanted. His obvious bemusement gave her added confidence.

Pushing down her own nervousness, she stepped closer. She knew he was attracted to her. Even if his lower body hadn't betrayed him, his desire for her was evident in the way his breathing hitched when she touched him, and the way he stood rigidly still, as if he only barely held himself in check.

He watched her with an intensity that made her mouth go dry and her palms go damp. Her own breathing had quickened, and just the thought of touching Matt caused a whirlwind of heated sensation to swirl through her. The urge to feel his skin beneath her fingers was an overwhelming compulsion that she couldn't resist. Reaching out, she tentatively stroked her hands over his arms, admiring the contrast of her slender fingers against the hard bulge of his biceps. His skin was incredibly warm and she could feel the hard play of his muscles beneath her palms.

"I'm here because I haven't been able to stop thinking about you, either," she confessed. She swallowed hard and allowed her hands to travel upward, over his shoulders. She ran the back of her knuckles along the strong column of his throat before boldly cupping his jaw in the palms of her hands. "I'm here because you asked me to come."

Matt closed his eyes briefly and turned his face into her hand. His lips brushed over the sensitive center of her palm, and Megan felt a tremble go through his body. "You barely know me," he muttered against her skin.

"Not true," she protested, smoothing her thumbs over the faint stubble on his jaw. "I got to know you through your letters and phone calls. And what I know, I happen to like. A lot."

Matt's eyes burned into hers as he cupped her elbows and drew her just a little bit closer, until her breasts brushed against his chest. "I'm glad. But I still think we should take this slow—"

She laid her fingertips over his mouth. "Shh. Stop thinking. We only have this weekend, and there's so much I want to do."

His pupils dilated, swallowing up the surrounding green and darkening his eyes. "Like what?"

"Well, for starters, I'm dying to kiss you."

3

HER LIPS were incredibly soft and moist, and there was nothing hesitant about the way she cupped his face and angled her mouth across his, sweeping her tongue along the seam of his lips until he groaned audibly and opened beneath her tender onslaught.

She tasted faintly of mint, and she smelled good, like summer flowers. The press of her lush body against his was almost more than he could bear. It took every ounce of his restraint not to grab her sweet bottom and grind himself against her, letting her know just how completely turned on he was.

He'd known he was in trouble—big trouble—the instant he saw her standing in the bathroom door, looking as though she'd just stepped off the page of a Victoria's Secret catalog.

Megan O'Connell embodied every fantasy he'd ever had, and the little white dress she wore only emphasized her feminine assets and made him ache to explore all the smooth, tanned skin beneath. At first he'd thought she was wearing some kind of negligee, but then he'd noticed the sandals and necklace and realized his mistake.

The plunging neckline and miniscule bodice barely

contained her full breasts, and he could actually see the faint shadow of her areolas beneath the fabric. And her legs... Oh, man, her legs went on forever, long and slender and golden, and he could almost feel them locked around his hips. He found himself wondering if she wore any panties beneath the swirling skirt of her dress, and his dick hardened even more at the thought of her bare, slick flesh.

He'd been serious when he'd told her that he wanted to take it slow, but with her arms wreathed around his neck and the small, sexy noises she was making in the back of her throat, he knew there was no way he could back off. Not when he'd dreamed about this for so long. Not when all he really wanted was to push her little white dress up over her hips, lay her across the enormous bed and sink himself into her soft, welcoming body. She was everything he'd ever dreamed of.

Matt heard himself groan as her tongue slid hotly against his, and lust spiraled through him. His hands slid from her elbows to her waist, and then lower, to cup her luscious rear through the thin fabric of her dress. He fitted her against himself, and she encouraged him by straddling his leg and riding the big muscle of his thigh.

Matt knew they were moving too fast. He needed to slow things down, but his body refused to obey. His blood churned through his veins and his heartbeat was an insistent pounding in his ears. With difficulty, Matt dragged his mouth from Megan's and looked into her upturned face. Her brown eyes were hazy with pleasure, and her lips were swollen and damp from the kisses they'd shared. Then the pounding he'd heard came again, and with a rueful laugh he set Megan away from him.

"I think that's our room service," he explained, and in three strides moved to the door. He dug in his pocket and thrust some money at the hotel waiter who stood in the corridor, and then pulled the wheeled cart of food into the room and closed the door. He was in the process of throwing the dead bolt when he paused, opened the door again and hung the Do Not Disturb placard on the outside doorknob. He shut the door once more, locked it and secured the chain.

"What's this?" Megan asked.

"I, uh, thought we could celebrate a little," Matt explained, watching as Megan examined the contents of the cart.

A bottle of chilled champagne and two elegant champagne flutes stood next to a silver platter of sliced fruit, everything from pineapple and melon to ripe strawberries and succulent chunks of fresh oranges. Matt watched as Megan lifted the cover from a silver chafing dish to reveal several pots of warm fruit dip.

"Oh," she breathed, inhaling deeply. "Chocolate. This one looks like melted marshmallow cream and I think this might be butterscotch."

She dipped a finger into one of the selections and Matt watched, mesmerized, as she popped her finger into her mouth and slowly sucked it clean. "Mmm," she hummed, her eyes closing in pleasure. "Definitely butterscotch." She slanted him an innocent look. "You should try the marshmallow cream."

Without breaking his gaze, Megan swirled her finger through the melted marshmallow. Matt thought she would offer him her finger, and he was really looking forward to licking the sweet stickiness from the tip, much as she had just done. Instead, she shook her hair back and stroked her finger along her cleavage, leaving a gleaming white trail between her breasts.

His eyes flew to hers to make sure he'd read her invitation

correctly. The combination of uncertainty and anticipation he saw reflected there told him he hadn't misunderstood. Making love to Megan hadn't been part of his plan, and a part of him—the old-fashioned part that believed women should be courted and romanced—protested moving so fast. He wanted her to understand that she was special. As much as he wanted a physical relationship with her, he was willing to wait. But he hadn't counted on his own response to her; his body was hot and hard, and more than anything, he wanted to feel her flesh surrounding him. He wanted to lose himself in her.

"Oh, babe," he groaned, "you're killing me."

She smiled, and then she did offer him her finger, watching intently as he wrapped his lips around the digit and sucked the remnants of the sweet marshmallow from the tip. Her breathing quickened as he slowly released her finger and then grasped her by the waist and bent her backward just a little.

"I've never been much for sticky desserts," he rasped, as he bent his head, "but I think you've just made me an offer I can't resist."

Holding her firmly, he dipped his head and stroked his tongue along the marshmallow path. She gasped softly and clutched at his shoulders. Her skin was hot beneath the creamy confection and the taste of her, combined with the sugary marshmallow, was intoxicating. He lapped the last bit of sweetness from her skin and then trailed his lips over the swell of her breast beneath the fabric. When he reached the small thrust of her nipple, he hesitated, ready to back off if she indicated in any way that she didn't want this. But when she gave a small sound of assent and pressed her fingers into his shoulders, he drew her nipple into his mouth, savoring the sound of her little moan.

He angled his head so that he could see her face as he

suckled her through the thin material of her dress. She gripped his shoulders, her eyelids half-closed and her lips parted as she watched him. Still holding her closely with one arm, he used his free hand to ease the narrow strap of her sundress down over her shoulder. The fabric of her bodice loosened, and it took no effort at all to push it down and expose her bare breast to his greedy gaze. Matt pulled back slightly to admire her. Her flesh was round and firm, and the exposed nipple was large and dusky. He stroked his thumb across the stiff bud before dipping his head to flick it with his tongue.

"Unh." Megan made a strangled sound of need, and then her hands were everywhere, stroking over his back and shoulders, along his ribs and over his hips, and then up again to caress the back of his neck and urge his head closer.

Matt complied, drawing the hard nub deep into his mouth and swirling his tongue around it. Her body shifted restlessly against his and she was murmuring something that sounded like, "So good...so good."

He had to agree. Nothing had ever tasted as good in his mouth as Megan O'Connell's breast. He rolled her nipple gently between his teeth before soothing the sensitized flesh with his tongue.

"I want to see you," she said raggedly, and used both hands to yank the hem of his T-shirt from the waistband of his trousers. Then her soft, warm palms slid beneath the fabric and smoothed over the bare skin of his ribs and chest.

Matt groaned and broke away long enough to reach behind his shoulders and grasp a fist full of his shirt and drag it over his head. He would have immediately returned to worshipping Megan's breast, but she stopped him with one hand in the center of his chest.

"I *really* want to see you," she said breathlessly, and leaned slightly back to look at him.

Matt's breath caught as Megan devoured him with her eyes, gratified that he'd kept himself in shape. Her gaze lingered on the black tribal tattoo that curved over his shoulder and extended downward along his upper arm. When she took in the rest of him, her expression was one of pure, female desire. He took the opportunity to slide a finger under the remaining strap of her dress and slip it over her shoulder until the entire bodice fell to her waist.

Her breasts gleamed softly in the muted light, and her thrusting nipples begged for his touch. His balls tightened and a shaft of pure lust jackknifed through his midsection.

"Oh, man," he said reverently, cupping each breast and testing their weight in his palms, "you are so damned beautiful. How did I get so lucky?"

"You haven't. At least, not yet." She smiled, smoothing her hands over his pectorals, and circling the small, hard nubs with her fingertips. "I wonder if you taste as good as you look?"

Before Matt could guess her intent, she reached out and dipped a finger in one of the pots of fruit dip, and slowly spread the warm goo over his nipple. Then, as he held his breath, she bent forward and covered him with her mouth, her tongue moving sensuously over his flesh, even as she reached up and offered him her finger.

Matt closed his lips around her finger, drawing on it the same way he had her breast, and finding the dual sensation of her fingertip in his mouth and her mouth on his flesh almost unbearable. He closed his eyes briefly against the exquisite sensation, his own hands still filled with the soft weight of her breasts.

"Mmm," she murmured against his skin, "raspberry. My

new favorite flavor." She withdrew her finger and continued to suck and lick his flesh, but now she was working her way downward until her hands came to rest on his belt buckle. She glanced up at him. "May I?"

Matt realized she had dropped to her knees in front of him, and his balls ached at the knowledge of what she wanted to do next.

"Oh, yeah," he agreed, pulling her to her feet, "but not like this."

Ignoring her cry of surprise, he bent forward and tucked a shoulder beneath her and then stood up, holding her in place with one arm clamped firmly across the back of her bare thighs. She laughed and clutched at his back, her long hair tickling his skin as he hefted her more firmly into place across his shoulder.

"Ooh, caveman tactics," she said, her breath coming hard. "I like it."

"I just need one hand free," he explained, leaning over and scooping up the entire tray of fruit dip, "because I think we're going to need this."

Carrying Megan and the tray of sauces, he crossed to the enormous bed and put the tray down on the bedside table. Only then did he allow Megan to slide very slowly from his shoulder, enjoying the glide of her bare skin against his.

"I think you have too many clothes on," he muttered.

Reaching behind her, Matt found the zipper at the back of the dress and drew it down until the entire garment loosened and then slithered over her hips to puddle on the floor around her feet. Immediately, all the saliva in his mouth evaporated. She wore nothing but a pair of tiny white underpants that emphasized her lushly curved buttocks and long legs.

Before he could unglue his tongue from the roof of his

mouth to tell Megan how incredibly, amazingly sexy he found her, she went back to work on his belt buckle.

"I think you're the one with too much clothing on," she said, and sat down on the edge of the bed, pulling him forward to stand between her spread knees. "Maybe you can help me with this."

Matt's brain kicked back into gear, but he couldn't tear his gaze from her ripe, taut body as his fingers worked the lacings on his boots and kicked them off. Megan's hands had released the fastening of his belt, and then she popped the button free on his camo pants. She hummed her approval as he helped her push the pants down over his hips, and he was achingly aware of his own arousal, jutting against the front of his boxers.

He wanted to go down on his knees and pay homage to all the lush, feminine flesh on display before him, but when she slipped a hand inside the waistband of his shorts, he ceased to think altogether.

"I've been dying to see this tattoo," she murmured, and while she enclosed one hand around his stiffened cock, she used her free hand to trace the Celtic knot that adorned his hip bone. "Mmm, I like this."

Matt wasn't sure if she referred to the tattoo or his raging erection. She stroked her hand along his length, watching his face, and the sensation was so intense that he knew he wasn't going to last. He clenched his teeth together hard enough that his molars ached, and then pushed her hand away.

"Babe, stop." His voice came out as a low growl. "You're going to finish me if you keep that up."

Megan's face was flushed, and although she didn't try to touch him again, she couldn't seem to drag her gaze away from where his cock strained toward her.

"Then tell me what to do," she implored, her fingers

tangling with his. "Tell me what you like…and how you like it."

Matt wanted to laugh. What he really liked was Megan, any way he could get her. In fact, he was a little bit afraid that he liked her way too much. She might be a stranger to him in many respects, but being with her made him feel as though he'd finally come home.

"Just let me kiss you," he said softly, "and we'll take it from there."

4

LEANING DOWN, Matt cupped her face in his big hands and kissed her, slowly and languorously, as if he had all the time in the world. He kissed her as if he hadn't been sex-deprived for the past eighteen months. As if kissing her wasn't the prelude, but the main event. But Megan could feel the barely restrained lust that drove him, and the fact that he gentled his touch for her only fueled her own rising desire.

She knew she was taking a huge risk. Although he'd said he wanted to get to know her better, she had no idea if he was interested in something long-term. Something permanent. But she no longer cared. When he'd turned toward her from the balcony, she'd seen something in his eyes that made her believe she could trust him, with both her heart and her body.

The guy knew how to kiss, slanting his mouth across hers and tormenting her with the slick slide of his tongue against her own, feasting on her lips until she heard a small whimper of need and realized with a sense of shock that it came from herself. She kissed him back, gripping his shoulders and pulling him back with her until she lay sprawled beneath him across the enormous bed. She used her feet to push his boxers down the length of his legs, and he helped her by kicking them completely free until only the fragile barrier of her panties separated them.

Matt braced himself over her with one hand on the mattress, and Megan gave a little cry of surprise when he hooked his free arm beneath her and hefted her more fully onto the bed. Then he lowered himself until his entire body was pressed against hers, skin to skin. She hummed her approval and slid her hands over his back and lower, cupping his lean buttocks and pulling him into the welcoming cradle of her hips. He bumped against her most private spot, hot and hard, and it was all she could do not to slide her thong aside and bring him inside. She knew she was damp with need, and when he slid a hand between her thighs to cup her, she writhed against him.

"Oh, man, you're so wet," he said hoarsely, and then he pushed the silk aside and slid a finger through her slick folds to caress her.

Megan's hips bucked as pleasure lashed through her, burning and fierce. When he found the small rise of flesh at the top of her cleft and swirled his finger over it, she cried out and then bit her lip, not wanting to come too soon. Not wanting this to end.

"That's it," Matt crooned, encouraging her small, frantic movements. He eased himself up just enough so that he could look directly into her face, his focus unwavering. "I want to see you come."

He inserted a finger inside her, and then another, and Megan gasped at the sensation. Matt dipped his head and slowly kissed her, before dragging his lips across her jaw and along the side of her neck. He raked his teeth along sensitive skin beneath her ear, and then drew it into his mouth, sucking gently as he thrust his fingers into her greedy flesh.

His body was warm and solid against hers, and he smelled delicious, like fresh soap and tangy aftershave. The combination was too much, and when he pulled back to look down at her again the expression in his sea-green eyes was so sexy and intense that Megan couldn't hold back any longer. With a strangled cry, she convulsed around his fingers and her body arched upward as a powerful orgasm crashed over her.

"Oh, man, that was so incredibly hot," Matt breathed against her mouth as tiny aftershocks rocked her body. "Listen, babe, we don't have to go any further. Watching you come apart was amazing. So, if you'd rather wait—"

"No, I don't want to wait," Megan gasped against his lips, realizing it was the truth. "I'm sure about this. About you." She gave a small laugh. "I know how that must sound, but I'm serious."

"Good," Matt growled, "because I can't wait any more. I've fantasized about doing this." He dragged her panties down her legs until she could kick free, and then he positioned himself between her splayed thighs.

Still shattered by the strength of her release, Megan struggled to think coherently. "A condom," she panted. "We need a condom."

With a muttered curse, Matt reached down and snatched his pants from the floor, digging impatiently through the pockets until he retrieved a small foil packet. Tearing it open, he covered himself with hands that visibly trembled, and then came over her, bracing himself with one hand on the mattress.

Megan lifted her head and looked down the length of their bodies to where he held his cock in his hand. He was thick and long, and even after the amazing climax she'd just experienced, she found herself wanting more.

"Come inside me," she invited, sliding her hands to his

hips and urging him forward. "I want to feel you, all of you."

Matt groaned and fitted himself against her sensitized flesh, and then surged slowly forward, stretching and filling her. The sense of heat and fullness was incredible, and Megan shifted experimentally.

"Don't move," Matt commanded in a strangled voice, holding her hips still with his hands. "God, I'm not sure I can last if you move."

"You feel so good," she murmured, exploring the sleek muscles of his back. "I'm not sure I can remain still."

"Just give me a sec. You're so snug." His voice sounded strained.

He bent his forehead to hers, his breathing ragged. Then slowly he began to move, rocking against her in a series of bone-melting thrusts. Megan couldn't help herself; she raised her legs and locked them around his lower back, moving her hips to meet his thrusts. When he captured her lips with his own and slid his tongue against hers, Megan felt the tendrils of a second orgasm begin to build. Her entire body felt flushed and heated.

She opened her eyes when Matt pulled back and dragged her bottom to the edge of the bed, hooking her legs over his elbows, opening her even more. He looked supremely male, all thrusting shoulders and hard muscles, and the expression on his face as he looked at the spot where they were joined was one of pure, masculine appreciation. Megan followed his gaze, and the sight of his flesh disappearing inside hers was the most erotic thing she'd ever seen.

"You are so damned beautiful," he said on a low growl.

Gripping her hips, he withdrew almost completely and then drove into her again. His movements became stronger and faster, and his face was taut with desire. The base of his cock tormented her with each driving motion until she could no longer bear the exquisite sensations.

She cried out as her orgasm hit her, feeling her body clench around Matt's unyielding flesh. With a hoarse shout, he thrust one last time and then stiffened, his head thrown back and the cords in his neck standing out in sharp relief. He pulsed strongly within her for several long seconds, before his head dropped forward and he exhaled on a shuddering sigh.

Withdrawing from her, he discarded the condom. Megan scooted herself back against the pillows, using her feet to push the coverlet down and drag the sheet over herself. Matt slid in beside her and pulled her against his side. Megan went willingly, laying her head on his shoulder and letting him curl his fingers around hers.

"That was amazing," she murmured, sliding a leg over his.

"Pretty unbelievable," he agreed, and pressed a kiss against her hair.

Angling her head, Megan studied his features. His eyes were closed and a contented smile played around his mouth. She took the opportunity to study him, noting the strong jaw and finely chiseled lips. His lashes were thick and incongruously long for a man, and when he opened his eyes to look at her, she was struck again by the color of his irises.

"I can't believe you don't have hordes of women waiting for you at home," she said, tracing a finger along his collarbone. "I mean, look at you. You're gorgeous."

He laughed softly and smoothed a tendril of her hair back with one finger. "I'm glad you think so."

Megan raised herself on one elbow. "I do." She gave him a teasing look. "You're sure there are no former girlfriends back on the east coast?"

Matt made a shrugging motion. "None that I'd be interested in getting in touch with." When Megan didn't respond, he continued. "Being in the military isn't exactly conducive to relationships, and being a sniper has a way of freaking some people out. All I'm saying is that some of the girlfriends I had weren't all that supportive of what I did."

Megan absorbed this, silently acknowledging that in the beginning, she'd had some difficulty accepting what he did for the military. But she understood the necessity of his job and it had never occurred to her not to support him, completely and unconditionally. Slowly, she lowered herself back to the pillow.

"Hey," Matt said, propping his head on his hand to look down at her. "That wasn't supposed to be a downer. I had a job to do and I did it."

"You haven't really told me why you're leaving the military, except to say that you've had enough. Is that why you're getting out?" she asked. "Because you weren't getting any support?"

"No," he said quickly. "I got support from those who mattered. It's just time I did something different with my life."

"Like what?"

To her astonishment, he actually looked uncomfortable. "I have some plans," he hedged. "Nothing definite yet, but I'm working on it."

Megan searched his face, but his expression was shuttered. "I see," she finally said. Even during their correspondence, he hadn't been clear on what he intended to do once he returned to civilian life except to say that he needed some time just to unwind and consider his options. "If there's anything I can help you with, let me know."

"Well, maybe you can help me understand why you

waited six months for a guy you'd never even met. You can't tell me that you don't have men lining up at your door."

Now it was Megan's turn to laugh. "There's not much opportunity to meet single men at an elementary school," she finally replied, pretending the change of subject didn't bother her. "I don't really go out much, and most of my close friends live outside of Massachusetts. Not that I mind. I'm more of the stay-at-home-and-watch-a-movie type, anyway."

"I hope you'll let me come over and watch a movie with you."

Reaching up, she cupped his lean jaw. "Consider yourself invited. It's strange, but I feel closer to you than to any other guy I've ever dated."

Matt turned his face into her palm. "I feel the same way. You're not like any woman I've met before, which is a good thing."

Megan didn't want to think about where their budding relationship might go. She told herself to take it a day at a time. He'd just come back from eighteen months in Iraq and she'd been waiting for him with open arms. Any guy would take what she'd offered. Would he still be interested in her once he settled into civilian life and realized he could have his pick of beautiful women?

"I guess time will tell," she finally answered. Not wanting to pursue the topic, she traced a finger over the white bandage above his ear. "Can you tell me how you were shot? Was there a battle?"

Matt laid a finger over her lips. "We got involved in a firefight with some insurgents, and I did something stupid. I left my post and made myself a target. But I'm fine. Really. I don't want you to worry about it."

Megan pushed his hand away. "Why did you leave your post? You must have had a good reason, right?"

Matt hesitated. "Yeah, I had a good reason. But it's over now and we don't need to talk about it."

Clearly, he didn't want to discuss his injury or how he'd received it. Still, Megan couldn't dispel the gory images playing through her head. She shuddered and pressed closer to him.

"I'm so glad you're safe," she whispered, brushing her lips over his. "And that you won't be going back."

Instead of answering her, he kissed her back, his lips moving sensuously over hers, even as his hand began a leisurely exploration of her body. Megan pulled away, vaguely disturbed by his silence. "You're not going back, are you?"

He nuzzled her neck, catching her earlobe between his teeth and then soothing the area with his tongue. "Nope." He lifted his head. "But there is something I have to tell you."

Megan drew in a deep breath, bracing herself for whatever it was he had to say. "I'm listening."

"There's nothing I want more than to spend the entire weekend here in this room with you. Believe me about that. But something's come up and I have to return to base at oh-six-hundred tomorrow morning. I'll try to be back as soon as I can, but I'm not sure how long this thing is going to take."

Megan frowned. "What thing?"

Matt actually looked embarrassed. "Just an awards ceremony. More of a dog-and-pony show for the press than anything else. But I have to be there."

"Are you getting an award?"

"A couple of medals, no big deal."

Megan gave a huff of disbelieving laughter. "I'm not sure that's true. You must have done something pretty extraordinary to be receiving a medal. I thought they only gave them to heroes."

"Trust me," Matt said quietly, "I'm no hero."

When he didn't elaborate, she pretended to be absorbed in drawing an intricate pattern on his chest with her finger. "So, do you have family coming to the ceremony?"

"Nah. It was a last-minute thing. There's a four-star general visiting the base and the top brass apparently thought it would be cool for him to make the presentations, so there wasn't much time to contact family."

"But could you bring someone if you wanted to?" Megan persisted.

"Sure I could." He slid his hand beneath her hair to cup the nape of her neck and pulled her down until his lips were a mere breath from hers. "Listen, I'd ask you to come but I'm not sure how long it will take and it might be boring for you. You'll be happier here. You can go down to the beach, do some shopping, or just hang out. I'll be back before you know it, and I promise I'll make it up to you."

He captured her lips in a kiss that was both searingly hot and sweetly tender. His arms slid around her, one hand tangling in her hair while the other slid down her back and over her rump to possessively cup and knead her buttocks. Beneath her hips, she could feel him growing hard again, and an answering need began to build low in her womb.

But as he rolled her beneath him, Megan couldn't help but wonder why he seemed so determined to keep her and his military life separate.

5

FOUR DAYS LATER, Megan opened the front door of her town house and scooped the morning paper from the small porch. She looked at the two envelopes she held in her hand, both addressed to Sergeant Matt Talbot. She'd become so accustomed to sending him letters that even though he was back in the States, she couldn't quite get out of the habit. But these letters were different than the ones she'd sent to him in Iraq.

She'd deluded herself into thinking she had known him through his letters and sporadic phone calls. The truth was, she hadn't known him then, not really. She hadn't experienced what it was like to be held in his arms, to have his mouth and hands on her. To have the full, potent force of his attention focused on her. To lose herself in him.

Since returning to the east coast, she hadn't been able to stop thinking about him. A pleasurable glow from their weekend still clung to her and she'd written the letters late at night when she missed him most, knowing she'd revealed more than she should have given the short amount of time that they'd known each other. But she hadn't exaggerated when she'd told him that she felt closer to him than she had to any other guy.

Megan had had relationships before, and some of them had been really good. But in the end, none of them had worked out. She was ready to share her life—and her heart—with someone. With Matt. After their amazing weekend together, she was certain that he felt the same way. Now she tucked the stamped envelopes into her mailbox for the mailman to collect.

A breeze caught the loose ends of her silk dressing gown and swirled it around her bare feet and she paused for a moment to savor the salty-fresh scent of the ocean.

Her town house was located several blocks from the waterfront, but on a quiet morning like this, she could hear the surf pounding against the seawall. She'd been raised on the coast of Maine, within a stone's throw of the ocean. When she'd moved south, to Massachusetts, she knew she had to live within walking distance of the beach. There was no way she could afford the expensive homes along the waterfront, but her little town house suited her just fine, and she could walk to the beach within a matter of minutes.

The sound of the surf reminded her that she was back on the east coast while Matt was still thousands of miles away on the west coast. Was he awake at Camp Pendleton, maybe going for a morning run along the beaches of the Pacific?

With a sigh, Megan stepped back inside and closed the door firmly behind her. In the two days since she'd returned to Massachusetts, she hadn't heard from Matt. He'd said he would call, but hadn't been specific about when that might be. Did he think of her? Did he miss her? Or had he just chalked up their time together as a fun weekend interlude?

After their first night together, he'd woken her at dawn with his mouth on her breast and his hand stroking her bottom. She'd been shocked at how swiftly her body responded to his, how she could go from feeling sleepy to sexy in a matter of minutes. They'd made unhurried love, and then she'd curled up in the bedsheets and watched as he dressed.

"I don't know what time I'll be back," he'd said as he'd kissed her, "so don't hang around if you have things you want to do."

He'd left his credit card for her to use, despite her adamant protests that she did not want it and would not use it. As if she really wanted to go shopping alone, or have lunch by herself at some seaside restaurant. She'd flown all the way to California to be with him, and he thought she might have other plans?

In the end, he hadn't arrived back at the hotel until after sunset, although he'd kept his promise and made it up to her. She smiled, thinking about the little restaurant he'd taken her to and how they'd walked back to the hotel along the dark beach. When they'd come across a deserted lifeguard station, Matt had urged her up the wooden ramp to the covered deck, and had kissed her and tormented her with his mouth and hands until she'd all but torn his clothes off and begged him to take her. And he had, up against the wall of the hut, surrounded by darkness, with the pounding of the surf drowning out her cries of pleasure.

Now she placed the newspaper on the kitchen table and poured herself a cup of coffee, telling herself that if she didn't hear from Matt today, she would call him tonight. What she wouldn't do was get all freaked out about the fact that she hadn't heard from him. After all, he was discharging from the military and he probably had a long list of things he needed to do.

When the phone rang, she startled, sloshing hot coffee over her fingers. She flapped her hand in the air as she snatched up the handset, her heart rate already accelerating in anticipation of hearing Matt's voice.

"Hi, sweetheart."

"Oh, hi, Mom," she said, sinking into a chair when she heard her mother's voice on the other end.

"Are you okay?" her mother asked. "You sound a little blue."

Megan sighed. "I'm okay. I thought you were someone else."

"Someone else, as in someone male?" Megan heard the hopeful note in her mom's voice.

"Yes," she replied, rolling her eyes. "Matt Talbot, the marine I was telling you about. He's back in the States, but he's doing his out-processing in California and I was just hoping he'd call."

"You realize it's barely six o'clock in the morning on the west coast?"

"Well, maybe he's an early riser," Megan said, not wanting to tell her mother that Matt was definitely a morning person, or how she knew that little tidbit of information. "Anyway, what's up?"

"I wanted to let you know that Erin and the kids are coming to visit next week, and I know she'd love it if you could come up, even for an afternoon."

Megan thought of her sister and her three rambunctious nephews. She missed them like crazy. Being so far from her family had been the most difficult part of moving to Massachusetts. Unlike most of her college friends, Megan really enjoyed spending time with her parents and her sisters, and she loved playing with her young nieces and nephews.

"I can come up midweek," she replied. "Maybe I can take the boys to the arcades."

"They'd like that. Oh, and I also wanted to remind you

about the Fourth of July weekend. Will you be bringing anyone? Your marine, maybe?"

Megan loved the annual cookout at her parents' beach house on the Maine coast with her three siblings and extended family. Her dad and brothers-in-law always prepared a lobster- and clambake on the beach, and the day usually involved a rousing game of beach volleyball, bodysurfing and sandcastle competitions. After dark, they would build a small fire on the sand and watch the fireworks.

Would Matt want to come with her? She didn't want to commit him to coming without talking with him first. In fact, she wasn't sure their relationship was even to the point where he'd be interested in meeting her family.

"I'm not sure, Mom," she stalled. "I'll ask him, but he may not even be back on the east coast by that time. Or he may want to spend that day with his own family."

"Well, there's plenty of time to decide. We'd love to meet him."

They chatted for a few minutes more and then Megan hung up the phone and unfolded the newspaper. She took a sip of coffee and then nearly choked on the hot liquid as she read the headline: Local Soldier Survives Bullet to the Head; Hailed as a Hero for His Actions.

Even before she scanned the article, Megan knew it was about Matt. She quickly read the story, which provided all the details of the gunfight that he had been reluctant to share with her, including how he had rescued an Iraqi child from danger. The article went on to say that in addition to saving the child, he'd also provided protective fire cover to several other marines, enabling them to scramble to safety. The last paragraph said he was a recent recipient of both the Purple Heart and the Bronze Star.

Megan frowned, recalling how he'd insisted the medals were no big deal. Why hadn't he wanted her to know that he was receiving two of the highest honors the military could bestow on a soldier? It made no sense to her. Despite his denial, he was a hero in every sense of the word.

Beside the article was a photo of Matt, the exact same photo that Megan had first seen on her boss's computer at work. She understood then that Matt's mother must have contacted the local newspaper and Megan felt her heart constrict with longing.

Setting her coffee aside, she decided to get dressed and go for her morning jog along the beach. There was something infinitely soothing about being near the water, and right now she needed that. As she entered her bedroom, the phone rang again. Her mother, most likely, having forgotten to tell her something in their earlier conversation. Sitting on the edge of the bed, she picked up the cordless phone from the bedside table.

"Did you forget something?" she asked in a teasing tone.

"Oh, yeah," answered a deeply masculine voice. "I forgot to tell you how much I'm looking forward to seeing you again."

"Matt!" Megan's heart did a somersault and then exploded into frenzied action. "I wasn't expecting you. I thought you were my mother."

He chuckled, the sound curling warmly inside her ear, and she could easily imagine his face creasing into a smile. "Babe, I am definitely not your mother, and I expect she wouldn't approve of the things that are going through my mind right now where her daughter is concerned. How're you?"

Megan couldn't lie. "Missing you."

"Yeah, me, too. I wanted to call you earlier, but things have been a little crazy here. Today's not looking much better, so I thought I'd call you before I left for the base."

"I'm glad you did. The local paper ran a front-page story about you, Matt. About what happened to you over there, and how you saved that little girl. They're calling you a hero."

There was a brief silence. "That had to have been my parents' doing."

"Why didn't you tell me you were shot while rescuing a child? Or that the weekend I was in California with you, they awarded you the Purple Heart and the Bronze Star?" Megan couldn't keep the dismay out of her voice.

She heard him blow out a breath of frustration. "I was just doing my job, babe."

"Not according to the papers." Megan couldn't believe he was making light of something so important. "Matt, what you did was amazing. The tabloids are saying that you're a hero, that you survived that bullet because you rescued the child."

Matt snorted. "Oh, right. Let me tell you something. My surviving that bullet was sheer luck and had nothing to do with karma." His voice dropped, as if he was talking to himself. "If that was the case, I'd definitely be dead."

"Matt," she said, using her firmest teacher voice, "don't you dare talk like that. You did what needed to be done, and you saved lives. Don't you ever forget that, okay? That little girl's family owes you a debt of gratitude. You *are* a hero."

"All I can say is it must be a slow day in the newsroom if they agreed to do a front-page story about me." He gave a rueful laugh. "Not very exciting."

Megan smiled. "You're being modest. Besides, I happen to find you very exciting."

"I'm glad you think so." Matt's voice dropped an octave. "What are you wearing right now?"

"What?"

"What time did you get up?"

Megan glanced at her bedside clock. "I got up about thirty minutes ago. Why?"

"What did you wear to bed?"

Megan bit back a smile. "A pair of underpants and an old T-shirt."

"Like the one in the photo you sent to me?"

Megan recalled the picture she had sent to Matt of herself, clad in a pair of shorts and a cami.

"Not exactly," she replied.

"Describe it to me, then," he said, and his voice had taken on a husky note. "I dreamed of you last night. I woke up with a helluva hard-on."

Megan felt herself flush warmly all over, she could envision it so clearly. "What did you do?" Her voice was breathless.

Matt laughed softly. "Nothing. I called you, because this is something only you can take care of. So, describe to me what you're wearing. In detail."

"Are you still in bed?"

"Oh, yeah."

"What are *you* wearing?" Megan asked softly, but had a feeling she already knew.

"Nothing, babe. Absolutely nothing."

Megan realized her breathing had quickened just thinking about him in bed, naked and aroused. "I wish I was there with you. I could…take care of you."

"Oh, you will," he said huskily. "What color are your panties?"

Megan glanced down at herself. "They're pale blue. Satin."

"Mm. Sounds nice. What about the top?"

"It's just plain white cotton."

"There's nothing plain about it, babe."

Megan laughed uncertainly. "How do you know? You can't see it."

"Oh, I can imagine it just fine. I can see the way the fabric hugs your curves, and that plain white cotton does nothing to hide your breasts, or the fact that your nipples are hard."

A quick glance confirmed he was right; her nipples jutted out beneath the thin fabric of the shirt.

"How did you know?"

Matt chuckled warmly. "Male intuition. Where are you right now?"

"Sitting on the edge of my bed."

"Perfect. Now lie back against the pillows and run your fingers over your breasts. Go ahead," he urged when she hesitated. "Tell me when you're there."

Megan did as he asked, feeling a little foolish but recognizing the tendrils of excitement that were beginning to unfurl low in her womb. She felt naughty, but at the same time she wanted to find out just how far Matt might take this, and how willing she might be to go along with him.

"I'm lying back against the pillows," she said. "I'm wearing my silk bathrobe over my underwear. It's white with black Japanese lettering."

"Spread it so that it fans out on the sheet around you, then bend your knees and open your legs," Matt commanded softly.

Megan did as he asked, letting her thighs fall apart and feeling warmth build at her core. Holding the phone to her ear, she used her free hand to skim over her breasts. She closed her eyes, imagining it was Matt's hand stroking her body.

"Oh," she gasped softly into the receiver, "I'm touching my breasts through the T-shirt. My nipples ache."

Matt groaned softly. "Play with them for me, babe. Roll them between your fingertips the way I would do."

"I am," she replied. "It feels so good. I wish I could see you, touch you...taste you."

"Oh, yeah. I'm wishing the same thing. I'm picturing you spread out on that bed. Slide your hand over your belly and down between your legs."

"Okay." Megan did as he asked. Her breathing quickened at the sensation. "My panties are damp," she breathed, "and I'm feeling so...so..."

"Horny?" She could hear the amusement in his voice. *"Yes."*

"Take your panties off and touch yourself," Matt said, his voice oddly hoarse. "Then tell me what you feel."

Megan pushed her panties down and then kicked them free, feeling wanton and uninhibited under Matt's encouragement. She slid her fingers through her damp curls until she found her slick center. "Oh," she groaned. "I'm wet. I'm pretending it's you touching me. I'm picturing you, naked. I can see how hard you are, and I wish I could put my mouth on you. I love how you taste."

"Ah, babe," Matt said, his voice a low growl. "I'm stroking my cock, imagining how hot you look right now. Put your fingers inside yourself, then touch your clit."

"Matt," she protested weakly, but did as he asked. Her hips shifted restlessly beneath her hand. She gave a soft moan, and heard Matt hum in approval.

"That's it...oh, man, I wish I was there. I'd go down on you, lick you and tease you with my tongue. Then, when your juices were covering my chin and you were begging me for release, I'd take you."

Matt's breathing had become ragged, as if he'd just sprinted up several flights of stairs, and Megan could picture him clearly, his hand fisted around his gorgeous erection, stroking it as it swelled. The image was so vivid and so arousing that when she circled her fingers over herself, the inner muscles of her channel began to tighten and then convulse as wave after wave of intense, dizzying pleasure consumed her.

"Oh, oh," she gasped into the phone, shuddering. "I'm coming, Matt."

He groaned loudly in her ear, his breathing harsh. "Me, too, babe, me, too."

The knowledge that he had reached the same pinnacle of release that she had was both exciting and disturbing. Never before had she met anyone who could entice her into having phone sex, and then actually succeed in bringing her to orgasm with nothing more than his sexy suggestions.

Megan lay against the pillows, boneless and sated, listening to the sound of Matt's breathing on the other end as it became more regular.

"Hey, you okay?" he asked after a moment.

"Mmm. That was unbelievable."

"Yeah, it was," Matt agreed. "Now maybe I can actually focus on something else today besides how much I miss you."

His words warmed Megan. "When are you coming home?"

"I fly into Boston on Friday."

Megan sat up, pulling her robe closed. "That's in two days!"

"Yep. I'm wrapping up a little sooner than expected. I actually have a favor to ask you. A buddy of mine is holding a fundraiser next week for wounded vets, and I volunteered to help out. I'd love it if you came with me."

"Where is the fundraiser being held?"

"Out at Fort Devens. They're having a carnival or something, and it's open to the public."

"I'd love to go," she said quickly.

"You're sure?" he asked, and she could hear the smile in his voice. "No other plans?"

"Nothing that I can't change," Megan assured him. "My mom called earlier to tell me that my sister was going to be in town, and asked if I'd come up to see her. But my family always gets together over the Fourth of July, so I'll see her then. I'd rather go to the fundraiser with you."

"Great. Maybe we can drive up to see your parents and your sister the next day."

Megan's eyebrows flew up, and she was grateful he couldn't see her astonished expression.

"If you want to, that is," Matt continued. "I'd like to meet your family. I kinda feel like I already know them."

Megan had talked about her family in her letters to Matt, but the fact that he wanted to meet them caused a tornado of anxiety to swirl through her stomach.

"Let's play it by ear," she finally managed. "I don't mind going up to see them, but I'll give you some time to change your mind."

Matt laughed. "Not going to happen. But it's totally up to you. I'll call you as soon as I get in. Listen, I hate to do this, but I have to run if I'm going to make it to the base in time for morning drills. I'll talk to you soon, okay?"

Megan hung up the phone and curled onto her side, replaying the entire scenario and conversation over in her head.

He wanted to meet her parents.

That in itself was enough to cause her stomach to fist. Megan had the sinking feeling that while Matt might have said he wanted to meet them just to be polite, her parents would attach more importance to the event than it actually warranted and begin thinking of Matt as The One.

Worse, Megan found herself hoping that they were right.

6

MATT COULDN'T BELIEVE that in the space of a few short days he'd forgotten what a knockout Megan was. When he'd pulled up to her town house to pick her up, he'd been blown away all over again by the package she presented. Wearing a pair of white shorts and a little pink tank top, she looked good enough to eat and it was all he could do not to drag her into her bedroom and devour her. But she'd been so self-conscious and shy about seeing him that he'd given her a chaste kiss instead and escorted her to his truck. In fact, he couldn't believe this was the same girl who had met him in California and who had engaged in off-the-charts-hot phone sex with him.

He had a suspicion that his newfound celebrity status had something to do with her reserve. The local news channels had run interviews with him and had declared him a true hero. The more he denied having done anything special, the more they made a big deal out of it. The reporters he'd talked to had seemed genuinely confused when he'd told them he really just wanted to settle into civilian life and become a regular guy. He didn't want to be a hero.

He'd promised to call Megan as soon as he arrived home, but it had been almost a full two days before he'd actually spoken to her. The first thing he'd done when he came home was to contact the state police academy to confirm his appointment to take the cadet entry exam. He'd done his homework, and he knew he'd be a perfect fit for their special tactical unit. He just needed to pass the exam. Hell, just passing wouldn't be good enough. He needed to ace the exam and then make a favorable impression during the interview.

He'd planned this for nearly a year, ever since he'd made the decision to leave the military. He'd carried a study guide with him even when he'd been in Iraq, and he had spent every spare minute preparing for the exam. He was as ready as he would ever be. There would be hundreds of applicants but only a fraction would be admitted to the academy. He intended to be one of them. Then there would be the long, rigorous months of recruit training, when he'd be required to live at the academy, much like boot camp.

He'd wanted to tell Megan about his plans, but had decided to wait until after the exam. He didn't want her to know just how much he wanted this. If, for some reason, he didn't get accepted into the academy, he didn't want to see her disappointment. Didn't want her to see *his* disappointment. And if he did pass the exam and get accepted, he'd surprise her and take her out for a special celebration.

After he'd confirmed his schedule to take the exam, he'd had to face the publicity that his return had elicited. It seemed to him that half the town had turned out for his homecoming, and his parents' house had been besieged by reporters and television crews eager to hear his story.

They wanted to see his damaged helmet, proof of the bullet that should have killed him but had merely grazed his scalp. They wanted to hear about the attack on the convoy, and how he had risked his life to rescue the child. Over the course of two days, the media had been unrelenting in their siege of him, his family and his neighbors, wanting to know every detail of his experience in Iraq.

What they didn't want to hear, and what Matt wasn't about to tell them, was how vulnerable he'd felt since he'd come home. He felt naked each time he went out in public without his weapon. Twice while driving, when other cars had come too close to his, he'd had to exercise every bit of physical restraint he had not to ram their vehicles. These weren't insurgents with improvised explosive devices; they were merely distracted drivers.

He wondered if the media would hail him as a hero if they knew he spent most of his nights standing at his bedroom window, scanning the surrounding trees for signs of the enemy, a habit he couldn't seem to break. He'd wanted to come home, so why did he feel so out of place?

He just wanted to spend some quality time with Megan. When he'd finally managed to reach her by phone, she'd sounded so prim and polite that he'd kept the conversation short. He didn't blame her for being annoyed with him. He'd been home for more than two days and hadn't called her; he knew women hated that shit. He'd make it up to her.

As they drove toward Fort Devens in his pickup truck, he couldn't help but steal glances at her beside him in the passenger seat. She'd pulled her honey-colored hair up into a loose knot, and tendrils escaped to tease her neck and cheeks. Looking over at him, she intercepted his gaze, and he watched as the tips of her ears turned pink.

"Sorry," he said with a grin. "I can't stop looking at you."

"Keep your eyes on the road, big guy," she chided, but smiled back at him, clearly pleased. "So how does it feel to be home? I mean, really home?"

"Strange, actually. I haven't lived in my parents' house in a long time. I'm having trouble sleeping."

"Maybe that's just the time change," Megan suggested. "Or the fact that you're not in your usual bed."

"You mean a hole dug into the dirt?" Matt glanced at her, wondering how much he should reveal. "I've been having nightmares."

"Considering what you've been through, that doesn't surprise me. Do you want to talk about them?" she asked quietly.

Matt's knuckles tightened on the steering wheel. Did he want to talk about them? Hell, no. But maybe if he told her about the nightmares, the horror of them would fade a little bit.

"I'm back in Iraq," he finally said, "in the middle of that gunfight, and this time I don't make it to the little girl in time."

Reaching across the seat, Megan covered his hand with hers. "But you did make it in time, Matt, and you saved her. I'm sure your nightmares are normal, considering what you've been through. You survived a traumatic event. Now you just need to let yourself recover."

Matt gave her a rueful smile. "You sound just like the shrink at Camp Pendleton."

"You can talk to me about anything. You know that, right?" Her eyes were concerned and earnest. "Anything, Matt. I'm not squeamish, and I would never make any judgments about what you did. What you *had* to do."

Matt felt something shift in his chest, and he squeezed her fingers. "Thanks, but I'm good."

"I know you're good." She smiled. "But I just want you to know that I'm here if you need me."

He nodded. "I do know, and it means a lot to me."

"The news reports said you had more than fifty

confirmed…hits," she said quietly. "I can't imagine what it must have been like for you, knowing that every time you went out, it was a life-or-death situation."

Matt squinted hard at the road. Aside from his mandatory sessions with the military shrink, he'd never talked to anyone about what he did in Iraq. He didn't miss the way Megan *had* hesitated before calling his confirmed kills *hits*.

"The number of kills a sniper gets doesn't really matter," he finally said. "It's not a game to see who can get the most kills. Like you said, it's a life-or-death situation. You have to be able to think on your feet, weigh the different possibilities for a given situation and execute the best choice."

"I know that whatever decisions you made, they were the right ones," Megan said with conviction.

Glancing over at her, Matt realized that she was being completely sincere. She wasn't just saying what she thought he wanted to hear. Her unconditional support was just one of the things about her that had captured his heart. He'd had girlfriends who couldn't get past what he did for the military and who had been unable to commit for the long haul. Then there were the women who had only been interested in him because he was a sniper—groupies who got some kind of twisted thrill out of being with a guy they thought was dangerous.

Then there was Megan. Sweet, sincere and oh, so sexy. He found everything about her irresistible. More importantly, he felt good when he was with her. Good about them as a couple, good about himself as a person. She deserved to know the truth about his decision to leave the military.

"I was a sniper for six years," he finally said. "But I'm not getting out of the military because I had a problem shooting insurgents." He caught her gaze for a long second.

"I'm getting out because I had no problem—none whatso-ever—in taking them out."

He saw the alarm that flared briefly in her brown eyes, and dragged his attention back to the road, not wanting to see the dawning revulsion in her expression. He jumped a little when she leaned over and pressed her face to his shoulder.

"Oh, Matt," she said, her voice muffled against his arm. "Pull the truck over, please."

Grimacing, Matt hauled the vehicle over to the break-down lane and thrust it into Park. He held both hands on the steering wheel while Megan sniffled against his shoulder.

Finally, she lifted her head. Catching his jaw in her hand, she forced him to look at her. What he saw in her face nearly undid him. There was no disgust or horror reflected there, only compassion and an understanding that caused his chest to constrict. Her eyes were moist, and he realized with a sense of wonder that she was crying for *him*.

"Matt, you're a professional soldier," she said firmly. "But that doesn't mean you're a cold-blooded killer. I don't believe you enjoy killing people. You did what you had to do." She stroked his jaw with her thumb. "But those days are behind you now. You served with honor and distinction and you have every reason to be proud of the service you provided. I know I'm proud of you."

"Megan." Her name came out on a half laugh, half groan, and then his arms were around her. He pulled her fully across the seat and buried his face in her neck, breath-ing in her clean, sweet scent. She responded by winding her arms around him and hugging him tight, even as she pressed warm kisses against his neck and ear.

"I think you're an amazing man," she whispered, and

then she found his mouth with her own, kissing him fervently.

Matt groaned and slanted his lips hard across hers, wanting to absorb her, wanting to make her a part of himself. She made a small murmur of pleasure and shifted closer, and Matt deepened the kiss. He slid his tongue against hers and explored the sweet recesses of her mouth, aware that he was rock hard and throbbing with need. He found her breast with one hand and gently kneaded the firm flesh, loving how her nipple beaded against his palm.

"Oh, man," he breathed against her mouth, "everything about you turns me on. I think about you all the time, and I've been dying to be with you again."

"Me, too," Megan whispered, and arched against his hand. "I've been thinking, too, that maybe you'd sleep better if you had company at night."

Matt laughed softly. "I'm not sure my mother would approve of my having a sleepover under her roof."

"What if you moved in with me?"

Matt stilled. Slowly, he pulled back and searched Megan's face. She chewed her lower lip, and he saw the apprehension in her eyes.

"You're asking me to move in with you?" he repeated lamely.

"Well, only if you want to. I know it's fast, but I have the room, and—"

"Won't that be awkward for you at work? I mean, sleeping with the boss's son?" He couldn't prevent the smile that tugged at his mouth.

"Would it be awkward for you?" she countered. "Because I honestly don't think your mother would have a problem with it. We're both adults, and I think she knows how I feel about you."

"And how do you feel?" he asked, sliding his palm along the fragile line of her jaw.

"Like this is the right thing to do." She smiled at him. "This feels right, Matt. Maybe we're moving too fast, but I feel as if I've known you forever, and I'd really like you to move in with me."

"Oh, man," he said softly, "I'd really like that, too."

To his surprise, he realized it was the truth. He liked the thought of living with Megan. He imagined what it would be like to take her to bed every night and wake up with her in his arms each morning. Then he remembered that if he was accepted into the state police academy, he'd be required to live on campus for six months of recruit training. He didn't want to reveal that bit of information to Megan. Not yet. Not until it was a sure thing.

"What's wrong?" she asked.

"Nothing," he assured her. "It's just that I can't really commit to moving in with you just yet. I want to, I really do, but I have a few things that I need to sort out first, okay?"

"Okay." She nodded, but Matt didn't miss the quick flare of disappointment in her eyes, quickly hidden by a smile. "The offer is open, so whenever you're ready, just let me know."

Matt kissed her once more before putting the truck into gear and pulling back out onto the highway. His thoughts were consumed with her offer, and what it would mean. He'd be committed to her, and the thought scared the hell out of him as much as it thrilled him.

He was quiet for the rest of the drive, although Megan didn't seem to notice. She kept up a steady flow of conversation, keeping it light. He enjoyed listening to her talk about everything from her job to spending summers on the coast of Maine with her three sisters. He could easily envision her as a towheaded child, running wild on the beach. Unbidden, he had a sudden image of what their own little girl might look like running across the sand. Almost immediately, he did a mental recoil.

Where the hell had *that* come from?

Sure, Megan was smart and sexy and gorgeous, and they'd just talked about moving in together, but no way were they ready to make a lifetime commitment to each other.

Were they?

When they arrived at Fort Devens a long line of cars was waiting to gain access to the fairgrounds. Matt reached over and covered Megan's hand with his. Her startled glance flew first to their linked fingers and then to his face.

"Thanks again for coming," he said. "This means a lot to me."

She gave him a wide smile. "Then I'm glad I came."

"Me, too. I think you'll like my buddies, but if they get a little rowdy or say anything inappropriate, just let me know."

Megan arched a slim eyebrow. "You forget—I teach fifth graders." Her smile widened. "Bring 'em on."

SEVERAL HOURS LATER, Megan collapsed gratefully onto a picnic-table bench, thankful for the overhead canopy that provided some relief from the sun. She dropped several stuffed animals onto the table, along with a bag of kettle corn and the remnants of her cotton candy. After two turns on the Tilt-a-Whirl, her stomach felt a little queasy, and the fried dough she'd enjoyed an hour earlier now sat like a stone in the pit of her stomach.

"You stay here, I'll grab you a bottle of water. Unless you'd prefer a beer?"

Megan looked up at the young man who hovered over

her. "Water sounds great," she assured him. She watched as he walked away, acknowledging that young, hard-bodied marines really weren't all that different from fifth graders.

She was exhausted.

She'd spent the entire afternoon exploring the fair in the company of two of Matt's Marine Corps buddies. Almost as soon as they'd arrived at the tent where his friends were grilling burgers and sausages, Matt had been pulled aside by the base commander and asked to provide an interview and photographs for the local media. She had seen the irritation that had flashed briefly in his eyes. He'd wanted to say no. She had wanted him to say no, too, but understood that wasn't an option.

Her two escorts, Liam and Alex, had taken their job seriously when Matt had told them to make sure she had a good time. They'd dragged her onto every ride, had tried to win a prize for her at every midway game, and had stuffed her so full of food that she was afraid she might actually burst. Their energy and enthusiasm had been both contagious and unflagging.

From her seat at the picnic table, she could see that Matt was immersed—quite literally—in the fundraiser. The marines had set up a dunk tank, and a steady stream of fairgoers stood in line to try their luck at dropping Matt into the tank of water below his collapsible seat. The sign over the dunk tank read Dunk a New England Warrior! Liam had explained to her that New England Warriors was the name of a nonprofit group that raised money to support injured soldiers and their families.

Matt wore nothing but a pair of tropical-print swim shorts, and Megan didn't have to wonder why the customers were mostly female. There were groups of giggling teenage girls who had no sooner taken their turn than they hurried to the end of the line to try again, willing to spend all their money on this one attraction. Then there were the older college-age girls who flirted outrageously with Matt as they tried unsuccessfully to dunk him.

Megan watched as several women strolled by with their husbands or boyfriends, only to stop when they got a glimpse of Matt sitting bare-chested on the chair over the water tank. It was these men who, in a show of friendly rivalry, accepted the challenge and with a well-aimed throw at the target, knocked Matt into the water. This only attracted more women to the dunk tank, because watching Matt come up from the water, sleek and muscular and slicking moisture back from his hair, was a glorious sight.

Nearby, Matt's buddies were selling grilled hamburgers, hot dogs and sausages. They shouted encouragement to the girls who tried to dunk Matt, and made several crude jokes about him having survived a bullet to the head. They'd leered at Megan in a friendly way, had joked with her and tried to persuade her to take a turn in the dunk tank. They were as rowdy as Matt had warned, but Megan found herself liking them. Beneath their brashness, she sensed they were each genuinely good and caring men.

"Here's your water."

Megan turned to see that Liam had returned, carrying a bottled water and a beer. He twisted the cap from the water and set it down in front of her. Megan took a grateful sip and then pressed the cold bottle against her neck in an effort to cool off.

"Sure you don't want a turn in the dunk tank?" he teased, watching her.

Megan laughed. "No, thanks."

Liam threw a leg over the picnic-table bench and sat down across from her. "So how did you and Talbot meet? I didn't know he was seeing anyone."

"I actually met him through an adopt-a-soldier program at the school where I work," Megan admitted. "I sent him a bunch of letters and care packages. We got to know each other pretty well during the last six months of his tour."

"Wow. So is this the first time you've actually met him? I mean, he's only been home for…what, four or five days?" He took a swig of his beer and considered her.

"I actually flew out to California last weekend, after he got back from Iraq. We spent some time together then." Megan knew she was blushing, but couldn't prevent the heat that seeped into her skin as she recalled what they had shared during that weekend.

"No shit." Liam looked impressed. "You usually only read about that kind of stuff in men's magazines. You know…'Dear Penthouse, I never thought this would happen to me….'" Seeing the expression on Megan's face, he abruptly broke off. "Sorry. Bad joke."

"No, it's fine," Megan said, laughing in spite of herself. "I'm sure a lot of people are surprised by how we met."

Liam shrugged. "Not really. Matt's never been one to turn down a good opportunity, you know? But his relationships never seem to last." Then, realizing his gaffe, he quickly backpedaled. "What I mean is, he's never had time for a real relationship because he's always been deployed. But now that he's getting out, he won't be deployed again and I'm sure things will be different. I mean, you're different. Your relationship will be different. Those other women—ah, shit. I'm making a mess of this, aren't I?"

He looked so mortified that Megan felt a pang of sympathy for him. "It's okay. I understand what you're trying to say."

His relationships never seem to last.

Try as she might, she couldn't get past those words. She could envision the kind of women that Matt might have dated in the past. Exotic women. Exciting women. She picked at the label on her water bottle and tried to sound casual, as if she weren't seething with jealousy at the very thought of Matt with another woman. "Do you know Matt well?"

"Hell, we went through boot camp together. I was actually pretty surprised to hear he was getting out. He's the kind of guy who thrives in a military environment, you know? He's an adrenaline junkie—the more dangerous the situation, the better he likes it."

Megan's gaze slid beyond Liam, to where Matt had just been dropped into the water. As he came to the surface, sun glistened off his wet body, emphasizing his sleek muscles. He laughed and traded gibes with the young woman who had managed to hit the target and send him into the dunk tank.

"Maybe that was true once," she finally said, "but he seems pretty happy with his decision to get out of the military."

Liam gave a noncommittal grunt. "Maybe. We'll see. Personally, I don't think he's cut out for civilian life. The Marine Corps is all he knows. Besides, there aren't too many employers looking for people with his particular specialty." He shook his head. "I give him a month before he's had enough and decides to reenlist. If boredom doesn't have him running to the nearest enlistment office, all this media hype sure as hell will. I hear his commanding officer has been campaigning pretty hard for him to come back. Matt's one of the best snipers he has."

Megan felt her chest constrict at Liam's words. She didn't want to think about Matt returning to active duty. She didn't believe he wanted to return, either, not after what he'd told her about his reasons for leaving. She understood that he operated on a strict code of values and serving his country was something he felt compelled to do. But his job had begun to affect him in a way that wasn't good, and she gave him credit for recognizing that fact. She didn't want him to return to active duty, but acknowledged that her reasons were purely selfish. She already thought of him as hers. The last thing she wanted was for him to return to Iraq.

"Do you think he'll go back?" she finally asked.

Liam hesitated. "I overheard him telling the base commander that he has a meeting with some of the top brass tomorrow to talk about his options. I'm pretty sure I heard him say that he might be gone for six months." He gave Megan a sympathetic look. "Like I said, they really want him back. He's a valuable commodity."

Megan didn't look at Liam, afraid he might see how much his words affected her. For the nearly six months that she'd corresponded with Matt, he'd insisted that he couldn't wait to get home, to get out of the military and begin life as a civilian. Not once, even as his discharge date drew near, did he ever suggest he might change his mind about that. Part of her had wanted to believe that she had something to do with his decision. Now she couldn't help but wonder just what place she held in Matt's future.

"Maybe you misunderstood," she finally said. "Matt hasn't given any indication that he intends to reenlist. In fact, he told me he has plans."

Even if he wasn't willing to share them with her. What had he said? *I have some plans. Nothing definite yet, but I'm working on it.* No matter what Liam had heard, Megan couldn't believe Matt's plans involved going back to Iraq.

"Maybe it has to do with the calendar deal he's been offered," Liam mused.

Megan frowned. "What calendar deal?"

Liam hesitated, then swore softly beneath his breath.

"Damn. He hasn't told you about it and now I've gone and shot my mouth off."

"What calendar deal?" Megan repeated, leaning toward Liam.

A shadow fell across the table between them. "I've been invited to go to New York City to do a photo shoot for a military calendar."

Startled, Megan looked up to see Matt standing beside them, toweling himself. Her mouth went dry at the sight of his supremely muscled physique, and she couldn't help but stare at the strip of pale skin on his abdomen, where his swim trunks had slipped down a bit, revealing his tattoo. She swallowed hard.

"That's great," she replied, trying to sound enthusiastic. Inwardly, she felt hurt that Matt hadn't shared this information with her. A calendar deal was huge, and yet he hadn't so much as mentioned it to her. They'd shared everything through their letters—their thoughts, their feelings, their experiences… Megan had really believed they kept no secrets from each other. He wasn't obligated to tell her about everything going on in his life, but the knowledge that he hadn't shared this news with her felt like a betrayal. Neither did she relish the idea of having him appear on a calendar for the enjoyment of other women.

"Just tell me it's not one of those hunk-of-the-month calendars, where they make you pose wearing nothing but a combat helmet and a smile, with a rifle positioned oh, so strategically across your credentials."

"Well…"

The sheepish expression on Matt's face told her that was exactly the kind of calendar he'd been invited to pose for, and Megan felt her stomach clench at the thought of his image being ogled by hundreds of thousands of women. "Are you going to do it?"

He shrugged. "I haven't decided yet." Matt sat down on the bench beside Megan. "Listen, I didn't tell you about the calendar because I didn't want to make a big deal out of it, especially when I wasn't certain it was something I wanted to do."

"For the money they're offering, you'd be crazy not to," observed Liam.

Matt shook his head. "It's not about the money. I'm just not all that comfortable taking my clothes off in front of strangers."

He slid Megan a heated look that said he didn't count her in that number and she felt herself go warm beneath his regard as she recalled just how anxious he'd been to peel his clothes off for *her*. For an instant, she forgot all about Liam and the other fairgoers, and it was just herself and Matt. A droplet of water trickled down the side of his face and slid toward his jaw, and Megan longed to capture it with her lips. Her desire must have shown in her expression, because something shifted in the air between them. Something hot and needy.

Matt broke the eye contact first. He stood up, but Megan didn't miss how he held his towel low, in front his shorts.

"I'll just go change, and then we can leave," he said, and Megan watched as he turned and walked awkwardly toward the restrooms.

Megan and Liam sat in silence for a moment.

"Well, it was nice meeting you, Megan," Liam finally said. He eased his long frame from the picnic-table bench and stood up. "I wish you all the best with Talbot. He's a good guy. And about what I said earlier…" He shrugged. "It's obvious that you two have something, and he's not going to screw that up."

Megan nodded. "Thanks."

She watched Liam return to where the other men were

grilling burgers and hot dogs. She couldn't dispel the images she'd had of Matt, stripped down to his skin as he posed for the calendar. She still couldn't understand why he hadn't told her about the offer, even if he hadn't yet made a decision about it. Was it that he didn't trust her? Or maybe she was making more out of it than necessary. She didn't begrudge him his newfound fame, but she had a sinking feeling that with all the publicity surrounding him, Matt's life would never again be the same.

What if Liam was right? What if Matt really was an adrenaline junkie, who thrived on danger and excitement? He wouldn't stick around a sleepy little town like Swampscott. And when he finally left for bigger and better things, Megan knew her life would never be the same, either.

7

MEGAN WAS UNCHARACTERISTICALLY quiet during the ride home, and Matt found he missed her easy conversation. Instead, she gazed out the window at the darkening landscape, and every so often a frown would furrow her smooth brow.

"Hey," he finally said, covering her hand with his own. "What's going on?"

"I'm just tired." She gave him a swift, apologetic smile, but Matt wasn't buying it.

"Yeah," he agreed. "But there's something else you're not telling me." A dark thought occurred to him. "If Liam or Alex said or did anything, I swear—"

"No! They were perfect gentlemen. I had a fun time with them."

Matt brought her hand to his mouth and pressed his lips against her palm. "Yeah, about that. I'm sorry I abandoned you today. I had no idea that the base commander had arranged a media interview, and I definitely hadn't planned to spend so much time in the dunk tank."

Megan pulled her hand free and curled it into a ball on her lap. "I guess that's the price of being a hero," she said, but her voice was overly bright.

"Listen," he said, frustrated. "I already told you I'm no hero. I'm just a regular guy." He watched as Megan bent her head and picked at some imaginary thread on her shorts. She didn't believe him. "Megan. I didn't ask for this—this media circus, okay? I'd rather spend my time with you."

She did look at him then, and when she spoke, her voice held an unmistakable challenge. "Fine. Stay with me tonight at my place. Tomorrow morning, let's get up early and drive along the coast, just the two of us. We can even check into some cute little B and B for the night instead of driving back."

They'd reached her street, and Matt pulled up in front of her town house and shut the engine off, turning in his seat to face her. Outside, he could hear the distant pounding of the surf against the seawall. He didn't know what was going on, but he already sensed it wasn't going to go well for him.

"Megan…I'd love to do that, I would. But tomorrow's not good for me. How about midweek, or the weekend after next?"

"Matt…"

She looked quickly away, and he could have sworn she blinked back tears. Then she turned to him and her expression was composed. But even in the dim light, he could see her agitation.

"Come here," he commanded gruffly, and reached for her, but she put her hands up to hold him off.

"Matt, I know where you're going tomorrow."

His hands fell and he sat back, stunned. He hadn't even told his parents about his plans. He hadn't wanted anyone to know, in case things didn't work out. Nothing worse than looking like a failure when the entire community—including the girl you were totally crazy for—believed you were a hero.

"How did you find out?"

She dropped her gaze to where her hands were clasped on her lap. "Liam told me. He overheard you talking to the base commander."

"Oh." Matt was floored.

He *had* told the base commander about his hope to enter the state police academy. Tomorrow he would take the three-hour written exam and then meet with some of the academy staff officers for an interview and a tour of the facility. If things went the way he hoped they would, he'd enter the academy for six months of intensive training. His focus sharpened on Megan. Was that what was bothering her? The enforced separation during the recruit training?

"If this works out, I'd only be gone for six months," he finally said.

"Only six months?" She gave a disbelieving laugh. "Listen to yourself!" She took a deep breath and leaned forward. "I'm not sure I can do this, Matt. I've just found you. I'm not sure I can give you up for another six months."

Matt felt as if he'd been punched in the solar plexus. "Listen, I'm sorry you had to find out this way. I wanted to tell you myself, but only after I knew for sure that I'd actually be going. I've given this a lot of thought, and I want to do it. I *need* to do it. This is important to me, Megan."

Important to us.

But he didn't say the words aloud. If Megan couldn't support him in this, then there didn't seem much point in continuing their relationship. Something in his chest clenched hard at the thought of letting her go, but he knew he'd have to. He'd had girlfriends before who hadn't been able to support what he did for a living. He knew firsthand how that resentment could erode a relationship and turn it into something ugly. He didn't ever want to reach that point with Megan.

She blinked several times and swallowed hard, and he sensed she was close to tears. "I'd worry about you."

He blew out a sharp breath of relief. If that was her only reason for not wanting him to become a trooper, he could put her fears to rest.

"You wouldn't need to worry. I'd be perfectly safe."

She arched an eyebrow. "Oh, really? So the bullets wouldn't be real? They'd be rubber bullets, or blanks?"

"Of course not."

Megan's entire body seemed to sag. "That's what I thought." She turned blindly for the door handle. "Good night, Matt."

What the—?

"Megan." Leaning across her body, he caught the door handle, preventing her from opening it and effectively trapping her against the seat. "Talk to me, babe, because whatever's going on, I know we can fix this."

She stared at him, and this time there was no mistaking the tears that swam in her eyes. "I understand why you want to do this, Matt. Really, I do. I'm just not sure—" She broke off, her face twisting. "I need some time to think."

He searched her eyes, and for the first time he could recall, he felt real fear. "Megan..." he breathed, "don't do this."

"I'm not like you." Her voice dropped so that he had to strain to hear her. "I'm not brave or strong. I'm a complete coward, and there's a part of me that would rather say goodbye to you now than watch you get killed later on."

"Babe, I am not going to get killed." He framed her face in his hands, searching her eyes. "Not when I've just found you."

She nodded, but didn't look at him. He understood that she was only barely holding it together.

"Okay," he finally relented. "I get that you need some

time. What are we talking about—a couple of days? Because I'm not sure I can be away from you for any longer than that."

She hesitated for a fraction of a second, and Matt found himself holding his breath.

"My family is having a Fourth of July get-together next weekend at their house on Small Point Beach," she finally said. "Maybe you could come up with me?"

Now it was Matt's turn to hesitate.

"Forget it," she said quickly. "It was a stupid idea."

"No, no," he protested. When she wouldn't look at him, he caught her face in his hand. "It's a great idea, and I'd love to meet your family. It's just that—"

She pulled her face away, her voice resigned. "You already have plans."

"Yeah…I've been invited to march in the Fourth of July parade down in Bristol, Connecticut. I've already committed to going," he admitted. "In fact, I was going to ask you if you wanted to come with me and make a weekend out of it. This parade is the oldest Independence Day parade in the country. I'm told it's quite an honor to be invited."

"Then you should go," she said, but he could see her smile was forced.

"What's going on, Megan? This has nothing to do with my going to the parade, or even my being away for another six months."

For a moment, he didn't think she was going to answer. Then she looked at him, and he saw the sadness and regret in her eyes.

"Don't get me wrong, Matt. I'm happy for the opportunities you've been given, because I think you're an amazing guy and you deserve them. But I can't help but wonder…"

"What? Can't help but wonder what?"

She drew in a deep breath. "I can't help but wonder what else you haven't told me. I thought we had something special, yet you're making all these plans that don't include me, so what I am I supposed to think?"

He blew out a hard breath. "It's not like that. We do have something special. *You're* special." He made a sound of frustration. "I didn't want to tell you about my plans in case they didn't work out."

Megan shook her head. "That's just it—if this is going to work then I need full disclosure. Up front. I shouldn't have to find out about stuff after the fact. It's not fair, Matt."

Matt nodded. "Agreed. Now can we please put all this behind us and move on?" He dipped his head to look at her. "You suggested that I might sleep better if I had company. I'd really like to spend the night with you, Megan."

She bit her lip, and he could see the conflict on her face. "I need time alone, Matt. I can't think when you're near, and I'm feeling so confused right now. I don't know what I want."

Matt fell back. He knew that he could overcome her resistance and persuade her to invite him in. He was sure of himself and of her attraction to him. But he also respected her enough to let her have the time she needed.

"Okay, fine," he said, and retreated to his side of the truck and placed his hands firmly on the steering wheel lest he be tempted to drag her into his arms. "Take whatever time you need. When you figure things out, let me know."

He sensed her hesitation, and hoped like hell she would reconsider.

"I'll give you a call," she said quietly and, leaning across the console, she pressed a kiss against his face. Matt closed his eyes briefly at the sensation, and then watched as she climbed out of the vehicle and ran quickly up the steps to her front door.

Only after Megan had disappeared inside did he acknowledge that there was one very important truth he hadn't shared with her; he'd fallen for her—hard.

8

MEGAN LEANED on the railing of her parents' deck and gazed across the dunes to the beach, where her three brothers-in-law and her father were heaping driftwood into a pile in preparation for an evening bonfire. Several of her nieces and nephews ran through the shallow surf, shrieking in delight as they chased each other with strands of seaweed. Reilly, her parents' ancient golden retriever, plodded along behind them with his tongue lolling out of his mouth. The sun had already sunk below the headland, streaking the sky with warm shades of pink. In a few more minutes, the beach would be completely dark except for the occasional bonfire. Farther down the stretch of sand, several couples strolled arm in arm.

Megan sighed, feeling alone despite the fact she was surrounded by her entire family. Nearly a week had passed since she had last seen Matt, and the time apart that she'd insisted was necessary in order for her to get her head together now felt like an enforced punishment. She missed him more than she would have thought possible, and spent most of her time thinking about him.

Several times, he'd tried to call her on her cell phone, but she hadn't picked up. Twice, he'd left her voice-mail messages, asking her to call him back. Nothing about either of those messages had indicated he missed her, or that he even wanted to see her. His last message had actually scared her. His voice had been quietly grim as he'd said, "Megan, we need to talk. There's something I need to tell you. Call me."

She hadn't.

She'd been too afraid of what he might say. She'd been too afraid that her insistence on having time to think had also provided *him* with the opportunity to think, and he'd come to the realization that he didn't really want to be with her, after all. She'd told him she was a coward, and now she knew it was the truth. She'd rather avoid him than hear him tell her that he was no longer interested in her. That he was returning to Iraq and that maybe it was better if they just called it quits.

"Hey, you okay?"

Megan turned to see her sister, Erin, standing beside her, and forced a smile.

"Of course. Why do you ask?"

Erin shrugged. "You just seem a little down."

Megan gave a rueful laugh and turned to stare blindly at the sea. "No wonder. I'm quite possibly the stupidest woman on the face of the planet."

Erin pressed a drink into Megan's hand. "Does this have something to do with your military hero? Mom said you were going to ask him to join us this weekend. I think she's disappointed that you didn't."

"Actually, I did invite him but he had something else going on," Megan replied, and took a sip of the drink.

"Oh. But you'll see him again?"

Megan turned to face her sister. "I'm not all that sure he wants to see me again. I found out he's reenlisting in the marines, and it totally freaked me out. I, um, overreacted."

"Oh, Meg…"

"I all but gave him an ultimatum. Me or the military." She gave a bitter laugh. "He's been trying to call me, but I've been too afraid to talk to him."

"You really like this guy?"

Something broke free in Megan's chest, something she'd desperately tried to hold in check since the day of the fair, when Liam had told her that not only did Matt have a poor track record with relationships, but that he'd almost certainly leave her to go back to the military.

"I more than like him, Erin." Her voice broke. "I'm crazy about him, and I think I may have made the biggest mistake of my life in pushing him away."

"Oh, sweetie…" Erin put her arms around Megan and drew her close, rubbing her back the way Megan had seen her do with her children on countless occasions. "Maybe you should just call him. I'm sure this can still be worked out."

Megan pulled away, sniffling. "I wish I could be so certain. I told him it would be easier to let him go now than to see him get killed later on." She swiped a hand across her eyes. "How stupid was that? Here I am, letting my own selfishness get in the way of spending time with him."

Erin considered her through compassionate eyes. "Would you want to be with him, even knowing he would eventually return to Iraq or Afghanistan? Even knowing he might not come home?"

"*Yes.*" Megan's voice was fierce. "I realize now that his determination to go back, in spite of what he's been through, is just one of the reasons why I love him so much."

There was an instant of silence as they both absorbed what Megan had just said. Reaching out, Erin removed the drink from Megan's hand and took a long swallow.

"I think you need to call him," she said, gesturing with the glass. "Today."

Megan nodded. "I will. I'm just going to take a walk to clear my head, and figure out what I'm going to say to him."

"Just be honest," Erin said. "Tell him you're crazy about him."

Megan made her way down to the steps, aware of Erin's eyes on her. "And don't be gone too long," her sister called. "The guys will be lighting the bonfire soon, and the fireworks begin in a half hour!"

Waving her hand in acknowledgment, Megan followed the path through the dunes to the beach, grateful that her nieces and nephews didn't notice her. As much as she enjoyed their energetic company, right now she'd rather be alone. She'd spent her childhood on this beach, and now she made her way to one of her favorite spots, a secluded section of dunes where she could sit and watch the waves but couldn't easily be seen by anyone in the nearby houses.

She sat down, looping her arms around her knees. What was Matt doing at this exact moment? Had he decided to stay in Connecticut for the day or had he returned to Massachusetts to celebrate the Fourth of July with his family? Had he missed her during the past week? Or had he already moved on with his life? Was that why he'd left her the voice-mail messages, saying they needed to talk?

She groaned and dropped her forehead onto her knees, mentally kicking herself. She should have gone to Bristol with him and watched him march in the parade. She should have reserved a room at some romantic little bed-and-breakfast and made it a weekend that he wouldn't ever forget. Instead, they were hundreds of miles apart.

Again.

Pop-pop-pop! Farther down the beach, a group of teens

began shooting off some small fireworks, and the noise reverberated across the water. Megan raised her head to watch, then a movement from the opposite direction caught her attention.

A lone figure made his way along the beach, and Megan felt her heart stutter in her chest. Slowly, she pushed to her feet. She could just make out the large deck on her parents' house, and unless her imagination was playing tricks on her, it seemed that her entire family stood there, watching the man as he walked toward her.

It was Matt, but she scarcely recognized him in his marine dress blues. He looked bigger than she remembered, and heartstoppingly handsome in uniform. His white hat and belt stood out starkly in the deepening gloom, and, as he drew closer, she saw a vibrant display of multicolored ribbons and gold medals on the breast of his dark blue jacket.

She stood, unmoving, as he climbed the short distance to where she stood at the top of the dunes. His face was set, his expression inscrutable.

"Matt…" she breathed. "How—why—? I wasn't expecting you."

"I had to come," he said simply. "You didn't answer my calls, didn't return my messages, and there's something that I need to tell you."

"How did you find me?"

A smile lifted one corner of his mouth, and Megan felt something in her chest shift. "You told me your parents' house was on Small Point Beach. Wasn't too difficult to find."

"Oh." She cleared her throat, feeling oddly breathless. "Did you, um, march in the parade today?"

"I did. Then I got in my truck and drove more than five hours to get here."

He hadn't even taken the time to change out of his uniform. Megan searched his face, seeing the evidence of strain etched around his mouth and eyes. His jaw was set, and he had the posture of a man prepared to do battle.

"I see." She gestured toward his uniform. "You look great."

He didn't acknowledge her words, but took a step toward her. "I received these in the mail the other day."

Megan blanched as he pulled two envelopes from his jacket. Even in the indistinct light, she recognized the writing on the outside. They were the letters she'd sent to him after their weekend in California. Recalling exactly what she'd written in those letters, she felt heat wash into her face.

"Matt, I wrote those words right after our weekend together. I was feeling lonely and—and sentimental."

"So what you wrote in these letters no longer holds true? You no longer think about me all the time, or replay everything we did together that weekend? You don't miss me at night and wish you could wake up in my arms?"

Megan couldn't lie, so she kept silent. The truth was, she did think about him constantly and more than anything, she wanted a replay of that amazing weekend.

"Why didn't you call me, Megan?"

She looked away, blinking. What had Erin said? *Just be honest.* She drew a deep breath. "I was afraid."

"Of what? Jesus…what do you have to be afraid of?"

"I was afraid you were calling to tell me that you didn't want to see me again."

"What?"

Hearing the astonished disbelief in his voice, Megan sharpened her gaze on him. "That's not why you were calling?"

"Absolutely not. Although, I figured that's why you

weren't returning my calls—because you'd decided you were no longer interested in *me*. But then I had these incredible letters, which completely contradicted your behavior. So I decided that if you'd changed your mind about me, I needed to hear it from you. Which is why I've come up here."

Megan put a hand to her chest, feeling the frantic racing of her heart. "Wait—you came all the way up here so that I could break up with you?"

"No. I came all the way up here to change your mind about ditching me." Stepping closer, he closed his hands around her arms, pulling her closer. "I came up here to tell you that I haven't been able to stop thinking about you. I want you to give us a chance." He dipped his head to look into her eyes. "In case you haven't figured it out, I'm crazy about you."

Megan struggled to make sense of his words. "But you're going back into the military," she argued weakly. "I won't see you for six months, and I'll be sick with worry that you'll be shot again, or worse."

Matt was looking at her oddly. "What? Who said anything about going back into the military?"

"Matt…don't tease me. Liam told me you were going to reenlist, and you told me yourself that you'll be gone for six months."

To her astonishment, Matt began to laugh.

"I'm going to the state police academy, babe, not the military. I took the entrance exam and I was accepted as a cadet. I'll train for six months beginning in the fall, but I'll be home every weekend."

Megan couldn't help herself; she sat abruptly down in the sand, struggling to absorb his words. Her whole body felt weak with reaction. Matt was entering the state police academy. He wasn't reenlisting.

Matt dropped down onto the sand beside her, removing his hat and tossing it into the nearby beach grass. He watched her intently. "You thought I was reenlisting?"

Megan nodded mutely, searching his face in the indistinct light and seeing the dawning realization there. "I thought you'd be leaving, and that I'd have to go for another six months without knowing if you were safe, waiting for your letters or your phone calls."

Reaching out, Matt hauled her against his body, his arms going around her and pulling her into his embrace. "No wonder you didn't invite me in that night," he said against her temple. "You probably thought I was a complete jerk, coming home just long enough to screw you before I headed out again."

Megan tipped her face up to look at Matt, feeling a smile tug at her mouth. "Well, that did cross my mind. But you don't know how many times I've regretted not inviting you in that night."

Matt slid his hand along her cheek, caressing her jaw. "Me, too," he murmured, and then lowered his head to capture her lips in a kiss that was so devastatingly tender that Megan felt tears prick behind her eyelids.

When he lowered her to the sand and followed her body with the length of his own, Megan felt a familiar longing begin to build low in her womb. She wound her arms around his neck, arching against him, telling him without words how much she wanted him.

"Oh, man, I've missed you," Matt breathed against her mouth. "I want to make love to you right here, right now." He caught the hem of her sundress and dragged it upward, exposing her to the night air. His hand skated over her midriff, caressing her skin.

Megan moaned softly and twined a leg around his, urging him closer. "Yes, yes," she whispered against his lips. "It's dark, nobody would see us. Make love to me, Matt."

"I'll take care of you," he said hoarsely. Using his body to shield her from anyone who might venture too close, he slid a hand beneath the edge of her panties and explored her slippery cleft.

"You're so wet," he groaned, circling his fingers over her. "I want to make you come. I've dreamed of doing this since that morning when I called you on the phone. Do you remember?"

The touch of his fingers against her slick flesh was an unbearable torment, and Megan let her legs fall apart, pushing against his hand. "Yes," she panted. "I remember."

Then he eased a finger inside her and Megan's back arched off the ground. She clenched her teeth hard in order not to cry out with pleasure.

"That's it," Matt growled in low approval, and slanted his mouth hard across hers, mating his tongue with her own as he worked magic with his hand. When he circled her clitoris with his thumb, and thrust with his fingers, Megan's reaction was immediate. Her body clamped down hard as a powerful orgasm crashed over her, shocking her with its swiftness. Brilliant lights flashed behind her closed eyelids and deafening noise filled her ears.

"Talk about perfect timing," Matt said, laughter in his voice. "That was amazing."

Megan opened her eyes. Behind Matt's head, a dazzling display of fireworks lit up the night sky. Matt smoothed her clothing into place before lying back on the sand and pulling her into his arms so that she lay cushioned on his chest.

Another burst of vibrant color shattered the darkness, but Megan scarcely noticed; she was too busy watching Matt's face.

"I could take care of you, too," she said softly, tracing a finger down his lean jaw.

Matt turned to look at her and even in the dim light, Megan could see the heat that flared in his eyes. "I'd love that, but I'm going to need a little more privacy for what I have in mind."

"You can spend the night at my parents' house," Megan said. "There's a guest room over the garage that nobody uses. I'll put fresh sheets on the bed and open the windows, and it should be fine."

"What about you? Where will you sleep?"

Megan smiled and pressed closer to him, sliding one leg over his thighs. "I'll bunk with my nieces, at least until they fall asleep."

"And then?"

"And then I'm all yours."

"I like the sound of that." Matt covered her mouth with his and kissed her until they were both breathless. He pulled away first. "So you're okay with my going to the police academy?"

Megan gave a burst of laughter. "Are you kidding? I'm more than okay with it, Matt. I'm thrilled. For you and for us. But I will miss you while you're doing your six months of training."

"You can always send me care packages," he said, his voice rich with suggestion. "We'll have the weekends to make up for lost time. And this time, there won't be anything to distract me. No media blitzes, no parades and no calendar shoots. I turned that offer down, by the way. I'm done being a hero."

"That's where you're wrong," Megan said. "You see, you'll always be my hero."

Matt smiled and braced himself on one elbow over her,

smoothing her hair back from her face. "I definitely like the sound of that."

Overhead, fireworks exploded in blooms of brilliant color, reflecting on the water and briefly illuminating their bodies, but, entwined together in the dunes, neither of them noticed.

* * * * *

COMING NEXT MONTH

Available July 27, 2010

#555 TWICE THE TEMPTATION
Cara Summers
Forbidden Fantasies/Encounters

#556 CLAIMED!
Vicki Lewis Thompson
Sons of Chance

#557 THE RENEGADE
Rhonda Nelson
Men Out of Uniform

#558 THE HEAT IS ON
Jill Shalvis
American Heroes

#559 CATCHING HEAT
Lisa Renee Jones

#560 DOUBLE PLAY
Joanne Rock
The Wrong Bed

HBCNM0710

The news reports said you had more than fifty